Great Divide

Emily Kiernan

Thanks and enjoy!

Emily Kiernan

ISBN:0615993168
ISBN-13:9780615993164

Dedication:

To my family, because you are not the family of this book yet still have given me everything I needed to create it. To Teddy, because when I heard secondhand that you were proud of me for this, it meant everything. To Ryan, because I love you, and because the things I make are also, always, for you.

Great Divide

1

When she comes to collect the late rent, she will find the house empty, the floor wet. She'll have missed her fled tenant by less than a day, or so she'll guess from the fresh tire marks in the mud of the lawn and the orange peels caught in the drain of the sink, still ripe and holding their citrus sting. There has been a light rain falling all week, but inside something more will seem to have been washed in or washed out. *In the downstairs bedroom, already submerged, was a man's boot print made in some dark substance, impossible to wash away. In the kitchen was a plastered-over place where a fist went through the wall.* All over the house, water will drip from one floor to another in a deepening orchestration of dropdropdropping from the clear soprano of rain on the leaking roof down to the guttural swish of ankle-deep pools in the basement where the sump pump has long since given up the ghost. In the kitchen, the wood will have gone as soft as spring sod, and the weeping of the bathroom walls will be inconsolable. The idling of the truck outside will be an echo of one that has since moved along, the high tone dropping into the practical hum of the lower gears. *Inside, a set of eyes stayed trained on the house even as they slipped down the driveway and onto the road.*

The damage, all tallied, will be extensive. It must have taken time, but how could she have lived with it? She's meticulous in all other ways—no bit of broken-down furniture left behind, no last bag of trash forgotten in the back bedroom, the floors vacuumed and the windows washed—but why bother when you've given the whole place over to the dripping and the mildew and the mold? Maybe she's been gone longer than it seems—since before the rain? There has always been rain, if not so much. Could she not have noticed or put off knowing so long that the leak had become a flood and soaked into everything? No, she couldn't have lived that way; someone would have seen. But what then—what had she done that the house had dissolved so quickly in her absence? By what daily maintenance had she held it together, yet left no trace of her habits now that she's thrown them off?

After three wrong numbers taken from old emergency contact information and the bad advice of a bag boy from the grocery store in town, Lorna finally succeeds in getting a call through to the girl's mother in Mt. Shasta, hours to the south in California.

"You've got a mess left up here," Lorna says. She doesn't say her name. When the other woman answered the phone her voice was as clear and high as a church Sunday in May, and she said, "Shandler residence," (which is not her daughter's name), as if she were the secretary in her own goddamned house. Lorna has seen too many Oregon-Coast women move out of state to get rich and pious—which is to say she knows the type.

"I'm sorry, I believe you have the wrong number," says the ladies' auxiliary, "This is the Shandler residence."

"You're who I want," Lorna says, tapping her index finger impatiently against the back of the phone. "I rent out the house your family's been living in all this time, and the last one was your girl, Jane. Now she's just left off, and God knows that's not what I'm complaining about. But I know my rights, and no way you folks can leave me with a flooded house without recompensations."

"My name hasn't been on that lease in years," the other woman says, and her voice has dropped way down out of her nose. There hasn't been a lease in years, but Lorna doesn't say so, being unsure of the legalities of the situation.

"I don't give a shit about what piece of paper you put your name on. It was your girl that left my house with an inch and a half of water on the floor. Or don't you think you have a responsibility to look after your own anymore?"

There is a little pause before the woman says, "I can't help you," and hangs up, and by that Lorna knows she's gotten that barb in at least. She calls back a few times, but no one answers. From her kitchen table, Lorna can see the rain starting to drip off the eaves of the porch again. She thinks of the leaking roof in the empty house and shakes her head. "Can't fuck it more than it's already fucked," she says aloud to the empty room.

Jane stood in the kitchen, listening for the sound of the drip. She'd been hearing it for days now, a drop or two at a time, echoing down from the attic stairs or tapping onto the porcelain of the bathroom sink. It seemed to move around, to travel along pipes or through the empty spaces between boards, to find her wherever she was, sorting through the mess of her father's papers, or on her knees, scrubbing at stains she guessed were as old as herself. It must have been, she realized, many drips, to be so audible throughout the house—a network of cracks and failings in the creaking, battered construction. Still, since she could find neither the source nor the evidence of even one leak, she thought of them all as a singular phenomenon—one intractable problem to be solved before she could leave.

She'd heard it from outside this time, from down the porch steps as she was straining to force one more bag into the density of the packed car.

It hadn't been too loud, just a little 'plunk' on the edge of hearing. She'd tried not to notice it, but a minute later she had thrown the bag on the ground and broken the zipper, spilling sleeves and hems into the mud, and she didn't have any other explanation of why she might have done that. A feeling of impossibility settled down over her, thick and cool. She stomped into the bare kitchen and stood listening for the noise, which plunked again from nowhere in particular. Perhaps it had always been there, she thought, and the accumulation of her life's possessions had only served to muffle it. *When her mother and sister left, the house had seemed to yawn and grow. There had begun a long-lasting neurosis of finding—for a day or a week, longer—some corner of her home malevolent, frightening, alien. As a child, she had always dreamed of secret passageways, hidden doors, false bookshelves, candlesticks that could be pulled down to lead her into someplace new.* Around her, the cupboards stood open and emptied, showing the flower-print paper that must always have lined their shelves. Cleaned out, the house revealed its secrets. All week she'd been finding things she had thought lost or had never known she'd had: letters, unsent or saved, boxes of photographs or of childhood trinkets, some of them marked with her own initials, or Mara's. These things of her sister's— or, less often, her mother's—she always found in the strangest places, tucked into boxes of books or abandoned in basement cupboards. She wondered if her father had meant to keep these reminders or if they had been somehow passed over when the house was purged. The arraignments seemed too purposeful, too well hidden; she felt a kind of new understanding, a dangerous note of forgiveness. She believed he had wanted these things.

At times, she had felt she was wandering through a museum, and each forgotten item reached her through waves of nostalgia or revelation. Other times it had felt like an estate sale, a set of clues that led only to a scavenger understanding. "Why do I have this?" she would think to herself, tossing another never-read paperback into the Goodwill box. "Who was I when I wanted this?"

Much of what she had found was inexplicable, as if it has been stashed away by a spectral inhabitant whose presence had gone unnoticed, somehow, for years. A parallel life, she thought, a ghost-self traveling the same ground. In the upstairs hall closet, a box of wrapping paper, neatly folded. Inside the cedar chest, a child's blue sweater, and a dog collar, unused. In the kitchen she'd found eight cans of noodle soup from a company she did not recognize. Some of the labels were torn off or faded as if they'd sat in the sun. She threw these away; she'd thrown away so much in the last week that it had become a kind of ethic. She felt filled up with the things she'd given over, and the harder the parting the greater the swell within her of something that was like pride and also like pressure: the pressure of water inside a cracked glass.

She wondered what would become of the other woman—the settled, accumulating one who had brought together the wild collection she now worked so hard to disband. Was that woman being dismantled too, Jane wondered, or had she soaked so much into the walls and the floorboards that there was no dislodging her? She thought of all the skinned knees and lost teeth the house had seen—twenty-odd years of hair and sweat and blood and bone. Her jaw tightened at the thought of how much of her was left in the corners and the cracks, at how many times she could be made over again from the remains.

Another drip fell from somewhere to somewhere else. It sounded as if it came from behind her now, near the door. She turned towards the noise but did not follow. It wasn't, she told herself, as if she'd be getting the security deposit back. What difference would a drip make in the damage and decay it had taken her lifetime to inflict? Looking out the door, she could see her father's shed, grown lopsided over the years despite the heavy wooden beam he'd dragged in to support the most dangerously sagging wall. The wind always blew right up over the bluff there, carrying water and salt, and everything on that side of the house looked petrified—too stiff to collapse.

The shed was still full of his things, sealed tight by the convoluted disorder of his projects and his attempts. As well as she had done, as much as she had discarded, this had overwhelmed her; she didn't have the strength to empty the place he'd possessed so fully. It was a terrible mess. From the ceiling there cascaded hooks and hangers dangling an array of rusted, useless tools or baskets filled with nails, with shards of glass, buttons, shells, swatches of fabric, or painted squares of wood. Sawhorses crowded the door, holding up half-formed table legs or porch rails—the fruits of the circle saw, which bared its malicious, glinting teeth from the back wall, too bright for the room. The walls, where visible, had turned a sort of nameless, sunless gray, but mostly there were only overflowing cabinets and stacked-up paint cans, some empty, some full. She'd gone in one night, drunk and armed with a thick roll of hefty bags and a bottle of bleach, but she'd been pushed back right away, repulsed by the sight of an old box spring shoved against the wall and torn open, filled with rats. It was all too much. She might as well have been inside him.

At a certain age, she had liked to sit outside the door and to listen to him work, the same way she used to lie awake, wishing he would talk in his sleep and reveal some secret.

In the end, she'd left it all the way it was, and though she left no note and made no calls to tell him she was going, she imagined that somehow he would know, that he would come back to inhabit the shell she'd left for him. She couldn't imagine the place without them—one of them at least. It seemed it would collapse in on itself. It seemed it would sink into nothing unless she or he was there to prop it up. The drip sounded again, trying, already, to wash them away.

Jane's phone rang from inside her pocket, and she answered it. It was Johnny, the only one she'd given the number.

"What's the hold up, baby?" he said. His voice was pitched high, pulling the words out slow and long. He was playing and excited. She'd grown so good at catching the movements of his voice on the phone that she wondered if having him in body would be too much for her, if she would get lost and overwhelmed in the conflicting currents of eyes and limbs and hands—the smell of him, and the taste.

"I'm almost ready," she said.

"Well, I've been sitting in the truck for a half an hour now, waiting for you to say go. If you aren't starting your engine in the next fifteen minutes, I'm going to go ahead and get a head start on you. You want me to get there first?"

"I don't care if you get there first," she said, and heard as his voice dropped down to somewhere deeper in his body.

"Hey, Jane," he said, "I want to do this right. I want us to get there at the same time. I don't want to be sitting in Kansas all by myself, waiting. The whole point is to meet you there. The very middle of the country. The big compromise. You're not going to leaving me hanging on this thing, are you?"

"Of course not," she said. "How could you think that?" But even then she could feel the house pulling on her. She would leave, but she knew how easy it would be to stay.

"Okay," he said. "Just remember there's a three-hour time difference. I don't have as much day left as you do."

"Okay," she said. "I'm trying. There's a leak in my roof I want to fix first."

"It's not your roof anymore. Get in the car."

"All right," she said, "okay. I'm walking out the door." She did not look back; she could not make this feel any different than the thousand entrances and exits that had come before, and she knew he wouldn't let her stop to try.

"Okay," he said. "I love you, Jane. I'll see you soon."

"I love you too," she said, but it got tangled up with the sound of waves crashing on the beach, and the shudder of the engine turning over, and the empty house waiting.

"Look, Jane," her *mother used to say as she caught sight of the water from the top of the drive, "it's waving to you." She'd always laughed at this little joke of hers.*

As she pulled out of the long driveway and onto the road, she tried to force a kind of reckoning. She wanted to wave to the world around her, the way she had as a child, fixing her world into place, even as she left it: goodbye house, goodbye trees, goodbye ocean, goodbye Jane.

"You're not going back," she said aloud, her voice too big for the tight space of the car's cabin—braying and embarrassed. "This is you now."

The air seemed to grow tighter then, to press more forcefully against her skin, as if making way for this new passenger—this unfamiliar and unapproachable creature she would try to call herself.

2

The last town you saw was miles ago, all closed down and shuttered tight for the evening, looking like it would never open up again. Like it was ghost town or a monument to sleep. There was a sign in a patch of grass, illuminated by a pale ground-light, and it said "Welcome to Drain, Oregon." You'd had to laugh at that. You think you'll just go on a little farther, stop in the next place big enough for a Holiday Inn, but you drive and drive and there is nothing. A density of nothingness. Finally, you find a gas station, just closing up. You knock on the locked door, and a woman with a wet rag in her hand comes and cracks it open long enough for you to ask where the closest hotel is. Another twenty minutes, she says. This isn't a place people tend to stop. You want to tell her that you know all about this, that you've lived your whole life in a place where no one stopped, and nothing stopped, and the whole world was just a little twirling orb you could touch all the edges of.

You hardly find the hotel, though it is the only building for a long way around. You almost turn back, thinking you must have taken the wrong turning; you can't imagine anything interrupting an emptiness so profound. Then the hotel appears ahead of you, like a mirage in an orb of yellow lights and each streetlight orb glistening and ridiculous against the darkness that turns it back before the bend in the road. It is called The Pauline.

You're shy about ringing the bell. You'd prayed for a night-clerk, but you knew as soon as you turned off the highway and onto the decaying macadam that there would not be one. By the side of the road, you can see the dark forms of houses fallen down and side streets becoming riverbeds. The place is in the process of un-placing, and so there is a bell beside the office door, and, you know, a bedroom behind the office, and an old television still playing softly in the three a.m. darkness. You ring the bell, ready to cringe at the mechanical bark endemic to old apartment buildings and places you are not welcome, but it is a newer bell, and more melodic than you expected. You listen for a moment, then ring again—too impatient—he opens the door almost as soon as you draw your hand away.

He looks old and doesn't look like anything else. You apologize and the man waves it away, filling in the necessary forms with a shaking hand that somehow writes clearly. You can't remember the license plate number on your car, and he follows you outside to write it down. His clothes are thin—shapeless and colorless, neither dirty nor clean. They were probably sold as pajamas, some long time ago, but have since aged into something less distinct: a uniform of entropy. You apologize for the cold, and he says it's all right, they need the money. You are glad you've brought enough cash, and you can see that he is too as you count it out onto the desktop. A credit card machine—the old kind that imprints the numbers on carbon paper—stands pushed to the side of the desk, unreliable, a concession already obsolete.

"You're a ways from home, I guess," he says as he copies the numbers off your driver's license into one of the notebooks that are stacked on the counter.

"I just left today," you say, and it feels far, but you won't show that.

"That's a day behind you," he says, and you don't known what he means. "Aren't they worried for you?"

"I guess they're worried for me," you say. You suppose he means your family, but when you say it you imagine something else—a flock of well-wishers, a flight of angels trailing out behind you.

"Well, you take care then. Then you be safe."

Above his head is a painting of a blond girl riding a horse, curly hair pulled back tight against her ears. The girl is grinning all out of perspective, her face too big above the gray horse's head. A photograph is slipped into the corner of the frame, pinched and folding where the wood has held it. The man sees you looking and gestures to the painting without looking himself.

"That was our daughter, Pauline."

You glance into the dark room behind the office but sense no human liveliness there. You can guess well enough.

"Oh," you say. He is still scribbling in the book and you wonder how long it will take. Suddenly you feel twice as tired.

"She painted that, too. Pauline. Of her horse and her."

"Oh," you say again. "She's lovely."

"She was an artistic type."

He hands you your key and tells you to have a good night. You go out across the empty parking lot and leave almost everything in the car because there is no one around to steal it.

In your room, you lie on the bed without bothering to undress or switch off the lights. You hate the feeling of being naked in cold, still rooms—their unfamiliarity a kind of threat. You have not traveled much in your life, except to visit your aunt in Eugene or to accompany your father on one of his brief and tiring vacations, but, even in this little experience, you have learned to go to bed with your clothes on and to discard them piece by piece in your sleep or your half-wakings. You spend some time fiddling with the heater, which roars, finally, into some kind of wakefulness, though the air that blows out of it seems somehow neither hot nor cold. It is like all other rooms. *Except, of course, your own room, where your dirty handprints and footprints had accrued on the wall by the bed, climbing higher as they grew in size, and where the sound of the waves ran under everything, always. In that room, you had once found a loose floorboard and hidden a toy under it, a little plastic rabbit, and had felt that that toy was always special ever afterwards, and then that floorboard always squeaked, and always woke you.*

On the wall ahead of you is another painting of Pauline's horse—just its head this time, a giant dark eye set against gray hair and a pale, cloudless sky. It is an ugly painting, flat and guileless, blunted shapes pushed into the outline of the thing they resemble—a horse in a bridle, reins dropping down into an unseen hand, a big blue ribbon hanging from somewhere just below the animal's ears. You look into it for a long time, trying to discern the inexpert brushstrokes, the organic forms so poorly described. There is a painting in every room, you are sure. You have stumbled your way into—not a hotel at all—a curated collection, all the remaining scraps of Pauline gathered into The Pauline, an exhibit organized by her own father, the leading authority, who could tell you all there was to tell on the subject of The Pauline, an artistic type, admirer of a bigheaded gray horse. You imagine him hanging the frames on the walls, just at eye level, or ordering the four-foot neon letters spelling out her name. Hers on the sign, and his on the lease.

You are halfway asleep, your eyes fluttering against the image on the wall, when you realize that the feeling travelling the front of your spine is hatred, a cold hatred for the sad old man and his dirty, stupid shrine.

The sun wakes you early as it comes creeping around the corners of the blackout blinds. You stay in bed for a long time after you're awake; the warm line of light that falls across your shoulder only makes the chill in the air more obvious. The heater has not heated, but the blankets are thick. Out the side of your window, you can see your car—an inch of snow on the hood but otherwise intact. You feel a gust of relief at this, and realize that in your dream it had been dismantled piece by piece by mice or creatures that looked like mice, but were really white balls of negative space or static that looked more like cotton than like mice. In your dream you thought they looked like mice, and they had taken your car apart and pulled it bit by bit into their holes, which were everywhere in the ground. You had used the phone in the hotel office to call Johnny, but he wouldn't answer, and the old man at the desk yelled at you for using the line too long. You sit up, and as the blankets fall to your waist, you resist the urge to wrap your arms around yourself, to rub your hands against your skin. Like getting into the ocean, you think. You just have to get used to it. Still, you

[15]

grab your jeans from the floor beside the bed and pull them on under the covers. You've remembered to bring your atlas in from the car, and you open it to the Oregon page. With your fingers, you trace the distance you drove yesterday and measure out the same distance ahead. If you take the 5, you might make it all the way to San Francisco, but you hate highways when the weather's bad and the trucks kick up all the dirty water from the road so you can't even tell when it's stopped raining. There's no reason to head so far south, but you've never been anywhere; you'd like to see. You like the look of the 101: a small red line snaking from the mountains to the water, squeezed between the forbidding blue of the interstate and the jagged cling of the 1. In places, the 1 runs so close to the coast that the black line of it on the map looks like some gigantic sea-wall built to keep the ocean from invading the delicate, improbable land—land willed into being by wild-eyed and blood-shot men with the unfathomable destiny of a century manifest in their faces. Cities growing in places horses die.

But the 101 looks afraid of the water, moving in close, then darting inland. As it should be, you think. You too are afraid of the water—*have been ever since you were eight and got knocked unconscious in the breakers, hitting your head on the bottom and waking up below with a vision of the world being ripped apart and scattered by the currents you viewed it through. Salt in your nose and your lungs. Your father fished you out and said the whole thing only lasted a moment, but you've always remembered it being so much longer, a dark stretch of time that did not need to fit into other time because it could seep around the edges or sink into the pores.*

It's not drowning that frightens you—you were a child, and in your disorientation you never imagined that you might die—but rather the sense that your hold on this place is precarious, which is a fear before the fear of death, and larger. You've known since then that you could fall asleep and wake elsewhere, to somewhere strange where the time you've lost comes back to you doubled and redoubled like a hall of mirrors and even the sunlight is liquid cold. You've never lived away from the coast. Maybe if you had, your fear would have faded or changed into the usual fears of childhood: abandonment or rejection. But where you lived the water came up onto the beach each night and carried things away, and from morning to morning and year to year the geography of your land changed. The dunes eroded, and the points softened into nothingness and then into absence. Your world had always been the thing at stake—not your life, and not your happiness, but only your besieged ground.

For a while after the accident you built sandcastles—or rather sand walls— digging trenches along hundreds of feet of beach and piling up the sand, pressing sea glass and broken shells into the wall as adornment—but only on the side facing the house. The side of the wall that faced the water you always left bare. Later you read stories about changelings and selkies—women who were also seals, or seals who were also women, always torn and always choosing between the ocean and the land. You made up

[16]

wild games, which you'd play for hours, standing on the shore and staring out, imagining your father as the prince who had stolen your sealskin, who had trapped you and kept you in your woman-shape to be his own. Other times you were the seal-self, swimming up to the beach, rubbing your belly against the shallows' sand, and looking at your house, imagining it a castle and you forever exiled from it. You'd wanted to dress as a selkie for Halloween the year you were ten, but your mother said you had to be either a seal or a mermaid, and you got so angry that you didn't dress up at all. Johnny laughed when you told him this and said he loved how obvious your psychology was, how it "floated on the surface of your actions." This made you feel dumb because you'd never thought of these things as meaning anything at all. You thought they were just funny kid stories.

Still, you swam every day except the coldest, when the inlets would clog with ice like curdled milk, and the air would freeze up so that even the waves went silent. All the while, you were afraid in a way you could never explain, to people who loved the ocean or to those who hated it. It is an intimate terror, the kind you cannot help pressing and probing, like the space left after a rotten tooth. You want to take the 1 and dangle yourself over the water, though you know you'll hate the drive, though you know it could cost you days.

Instead of choosing, you pull your black Sharpie from where you've stored it in the atlas's binding and begin to write the day's notes across the top of Oregon. It was Johnny's idea that you'd keep these journals. "For our kids," he'd said, and it had shocked you to hear him talk about that sort of thing. You'd been stunned into agreeing, and now the things you write come out stilted and strange. You've never thought about kids before. You cross out all the curse words, and then meticulously add them back in, hovering above your sentences, spiked on with carats. *You remember how you loved, as a child, to look at pictures of your parents from before you were born, to catch them in moments they could not know you saw.* You don't want your children to know that even now you have them in mind, have begun to imagine their features and to bring them into this moment that should still be covered in the wing-dust of the unknowable. Across northern Oregon you write, "Rain and rain and rain, circling Drain. It's a ^(fucking) beautiful nightmare out here. Woke up to snow. If that keeps up, I don't know how far I'll get today." You realize that you've made your writing too large, and your words have already strayed considerably south of your actual position. You stop; there wasn't much to say anyway. Instead, you flip to Pennsylvania, where Johnny stopped the night before, sleeping in his truck, though your sister Mara's house was only miles away. You'd told him to call her, but he'd been quiet and reluctant, and you'd understood. You stare at the spot on the map, crisscrossed with rivers and mountains—the place you met— then remember that you are angry with him for his unsentimental passage through that place that means so much to you still. You close the book. You don't want the kids to see you fight.

You'd asked him on the phone the day before if he would camp in the same spot the two of you had found together, if he would eat at the same diner, but he'd said no.

"This is about finding something new, Jane," he'd said. "We don't need any nostalgia."

You think you can understand this, but you wish he did not find it all so easy. There is a needling in your stomach that tells you he does not remember it the way you do.

Outside the hotel room, the sun is strangely warm on the back of your neck as you clear the snow off your windshield. Your feet are freezing and you wish you'd thought to get some better shoes. The engine turns over with only a token resistance, and you leave it to warm up while you return your key to the office.

In the daylight, the room looks abandoned. The sun coming through the window seems to shatter against the blinds so that everything looks covered in a layer of dust, or turning to dust, and you imagine it all blowing away as you shut the door behind you. The old man is gone. You stay, hovering over the counter with the keys still in your hand, picking what words you can out of the open ledgers and loose papers. You are not looking for anything in particular, but the looking itself sustains you. Among the names and dates, a few items draw your interest. In September there were several entries concerning something called The Rivers Board. A man called Drew was "disappointed" in March. The name Cheryl appears again and again, always crossed out, thick black lines snaking through the letters.

You don't know what you are hoping to see until you see it: a stack of letters on a shelf against the wall, leaning with the addresses half-obscured behind a jar of picture-nails. If they'd looked like he treasured them, you'd never have thought to touch. If you imagined he knew of their presence there—that they reached him as the rest of the cacophonous, half-discarded junk did not—you'd have been embarrassed to have even seen. But they were nothing: advertisements and special offers, the candy-colored last remains of every mortal thing. He could have thrown them away and had not—but nothing in the room was worth keeping, and it had all been kept.

You reach behind the counter and pick one up. A blue splash across the seal makes long-expired come-ons. You don't open it, of course. How terrible, you think, to get the dead girl's mail. How wrenching for grief to be summoned so cheaply.

But at least there is someone who doesn't know. Someone still affixes labels and postage. Someone still hopes for contact when all reasonable hope is given up. We live as long as we're remembered. For this week only, for six months guaranteed, the loss is not a perfect fact.

You are thinking of your father as you stand there. With the letter in your hand, you know you have outrun something you never had the sense to fear.

You set the letter back on the pile, and in doing so notice one that is not like the others. The paper is not the everlasting gloss of junk mail but a browning matte. The address is written in blue ink—an imperfect hand that pressed too hard on the P's. You pick this one up, examine the unbroken seal, and finally slip it into your pocket. You feel a sick twinge at this but do it anyway. This one shouldn't have been forgotten, shouldn't have been left to rot in this place. It had come from the world, from some real inhabitant outside, and it deserved to be carried back. You don't go any further than this in explaining it to yourself. The envelope is thick and stiff and pushes uncomfortably against the skin of your thigh.

The car has grown stifling in your absence—the heater is at least as old as the car itself, almost as old as you are, and it has no sense of restraint. You leave it on for a while though, stripping off layers of clothing as you drive, wearing the air like a sweater, thick and soft. Outside, the snow is melting fast, and the world is a water maze. Rivulets course down the rocky hillsides and pool in the potholes. When you cannot bear to breathe the car's air anymore and roll down the window, you can hear an incessant dripping that makes you think of a spring that is still months away, and you feel light, happy, and free. You want to sing, and do, loving for a moment your anonymity and your solitude. You resolve that this will be your trip and that you will call Johnny less than is kind. You are going towards him, but you do not want to forget that you are also going away— that you are going. You head back towards the coast; you will take your time.

After a while, you see that you are low on gas, and this pulls you out of what may have been an hour of musing. Maybe even more. You've pulled the letter out of your pocket and tossed it onto the seat beside you, though you can't precisely remember doing so. *You imagine him coming home to find you gone away with it, the lights out behind the faded lace curtains, and the parking lot empty of cars. Your heart beats fast—an unexpectedly thrilling little fantasy. You picture him noticing your theft, noticing it like you would notice the absence of an expected body in your bed. You imagine him knowing what you had done the way your own father had known when you were awake, even when you'd try to fool him, breathing deep and slow, your eyes held shut. Now it is your father you've imagined, and your house with you absent from it. His eyes scanning the little room behind the office where she had slept, from which she had abandoned him. His befuddlement, his dim understanding. What little was left of a daughter, hustled away into the waiting car, heading south in the brightness of a winter day.* You give the letter a little pat as you pull into the gas station, telling yourself, ridiculously, that Pauline has never been so far from home.

You get out of the car and stand as the attendant pumps; this is something you've always done, though you sense it is a strange habit. The attendant looks shy and gangly—sixteen, at most—and he seems to find your presence awkward. He'd like you to sit down, but you don't move. *Once, when you were young, your father told you it was disrespectful to sit and watch a man work, and you believe it in spite of yourself.*

"How far you going?" he says after a while. "You've got the car pretty packed up."

"Kansas," you say, and he laughs.

"You're going the wrong way," he says. "You want to get on the 5."

"I'm not rushing," you say. "I want to go along the coast."

"Not right now you don't. Didn't you hear about the floods?"

"The radio is broken," you say, pointing into the car. This isn't true, and you're not sure why you've said it, except that it sounded better than "No."

"They got a shitload of rain last night, I guess. The 101 is a parking lot. They might have it cleared up by the end of the day, but if I was you, I'd grab the 138 south to hook you up with the freeway. "

"Thanks," you say, and go to sit back in the car until he is finished.

3

You pull off the road underneath the sign for Mt. Shasta and sit for a while with your head resting in your hands. Every few moments you feel a new impulse wash over you, but before you can move to follow, it changes into its opposite or bleeds back into painful indecision. You open your phone three times, only to close it and drop it back into your purse. Once you get as far as dialing before abandoning the idea, and the call must have gotten through because Johnny calls you back a minute later, sounding worried.

"Janie, did you just try to call me?" he says, and you say, "Yep," and stop, knowing it isn't his fault, and still.

"Is everything okay?"

"Yep," you say again, wishing you could speak without the sound of your words echoing back to you.

"Why are you being this way, Janie?" he says. He is losing patience, and you wonder how he always seems to forget that this is what it is like to talk to you.

"I'm by my mother's house."

He is silent a long while. A compassionate silence.

"Are you stopping?"

"You choose for me."

"You know I can't," he says, then does. "Fuck her, Janie. A couple more days and you're clear of all of them. Just get back in the car and keep driving until you get there. Don't sleep and don't look back and don't let your father know you're gone and don't tell your sister that you've left and don't stop for your mother who wouldn't stop for you anyway, and you know that. I swear Janie, just keep driving and you'll be amazed how soon you can forget you ever heard their names."

Your heart skips because this kind of talk always excites you. It seems to require some effort from him to produce these apocalypses, and his voice has gone heavy and torn. It is a voice he gives only to you. This is how he won you.

"Jane," he says. "Jane, don't go. She's done nothing to deserve it."

"She might give me money," you say. "It would be the least she could do."

"We don't need her money. I'm good at being poor, Janie. As long as you have enough to get you there, we can sleep in the truck and eat out of the dumpsters, and as soon as I have fifty cents, I'll get you a ring out of one of the supermarket toy machines. What else could you want that her money could buy us?"

"The marriage license, maybe." You love it when he plays the romantic and lets you be practical and cool—it makes you feel strong.

"You'll do what you want, I guess, but I wish you'd just hurry up and get here."

"You're not there yet, either."

"I am. In every way except the physical. So you getting back on the road?"

"Yeah," you say, "I am."

Still, when you hang up, you sit for a long while, staring into the words on the sign.

It was more than the usual love affair between your mother and you, when you were very young and needed her so badly that you wanted to stay small and needing and forever under her care. The first thing you remember is lying in her bed beside her when you must have been two years old, or maybe three if she was pregnant with your sister, though you remember the line of her stomach under her dress, and it was flat. She was wearing heels, stockings, and a slip under her dress, which was white with yellow flowers hiding in the pleats. Out all night? Did that happen often then? You know it was morning because of the light in the room. Her room faced east towards the yard with the wash line, which she used in those years when she would brew sun tea and try to grow tomatoes in the soft soil against the house. Those were the very good years that you remember and Mara does not, and that is the great difference between you. In the three-year stretch between your consciousness and hers, there was a transfiguration.

In your memory your mother was standing, taking swaying dance-steps away from you, and you were aware of the music playing—Billie Holiday on the old record player that your mother had gotten when she turned thirteen and told her parents that she wanted to be a singer. You were quiet because she had told you about this song and made you feel that it was important in some wordless and unnamable way. You tried to imitate the expression that was on her face when she turned to look at you, but you must have gotten it wrong because the look vanished when she saw you, and then she turned away. All the while, you missed the smell of her, which moments before had been on the breath that she breathed into your face like pine needles and cinnamon cookies. You wanted her to come lie down next to you again and to put her hand on your hair and look at you the way she looked at the music in the air. You wanted this wildly. Bottomlessly.

"Can we go swimming?" you said because her dancing had reminded you of her swimming. She swam long-legged and slow in her blue one-piece bathing suit, the water making room for her as if she was the object and it the adornment—another pretty thing she wore. When you swam together, she had to stay near to you and hold her hands under your belly while you paddled, and so you liked it better than the dancing.

[22]

"No, honey," she said, still rocking her hips to the endless-slow rhythm of Ms. Holiday's voice. "Not now. Maybe when your daddy gets home."

It seems strange that he was not home, but then again this was years before things really went off the rails, and maybe he was working an early shift, doing penance for whatever transgressions he'd lately been caught in—swearing he'd never do it again. Laughable, of course; there were signs and markers. His capacity for penitence was one of the first things jettisoned from an increasingly feral nature.

"I'm tired, baby," she said, finally walking back to the bed. The song had ended, and she was quick and businesslike, click clicking heels on the floor. "Why don't you go back to your bed for a while? If you're a good girl and go back to bed, Daddy will take you swimming later."

You started to cry because it was the worst thing to be sent away by her, but she just stood staring and would not comfort you, and so you went.

You realize now that you could not really have felt so much intensity as you think you remember, and you wonder what you have embellished, and when, to suit the story that this one became—the long disintegration, the accusations and revelations that made your life into a ransom for hers. Of course, you will go to her. You could never have chosen not to.

4

She wasn't home when you arrived, something you hadn't expected. You remembered, inexplicably, the way from the highway to her house and entertained yourself by imagining the entrance you would make. You were happy in these thoughts as you jostled along the macadam that was decaying to gravel and then to dirt, your breaks whining on the hills, even as you shifted into second gear.

You don't get a chance to make a scene. Instead, she finds you sitting outside the garden gate. She must have seen you from the driveway. By the time she reaches you, her face is composed and impenetrable. Steve, her husband, had gone into the house a half-hour before, but you had said you preferred to wait where you were, though you felt like a petulant teenager when you did.

"Your landlord called me yesterday," she says. "She told me you'd left a mess."

"She's crazy," you say. "Don't you remember her?"

She just shrugs.

"I have groceries in the car," she says. "Will you help me bring them in?"

It's a terrible thing she does, acting as if she's always known what you would do, as if she has anticipated and dully expected your every coming and going, monitored every change of mind or lapse of spirit, and checked it off of the astral list of your doings, your fates. It's a conceit, of course, a common and unconvincing one. You think again that if she had ever just allowed herself to be shocked she would have been less complicit in all of it.

"Sure," you say.

Everything about her surprises you, but you quickly shove the feeling down. You should have known. Your mistake has been in imagining her so singularly—the mother of your first consciousness, the mother of the dance steps on the bedroom floor—when she is (has always been) a sort of woman. The sort of woman who buys organic strawberries for five dollars a pint at the liberal-themed and conservative-owned chain grocery, the sort of woman who has running shoes in the back of her car, and who is, at forty-five, still more beautiful than you, more lively, more glowing. On her walls, there are pictures of you and Mara—brawny, angelic country mice with horsey teeth and your arms thrown around each other, half-succumbing to giggles. The pictures are beautiful; the house is clean and cool. You begin to doubt that what was done to you was done to you, that this lovely, correct woman could have allowed it. It is a pleasant doubt—a refreshing oddity to feel wrong and not wronged.

When you turn around she is standing in the doorway behind you with her arms crossed, and her face is the intersection of defiance and regret. *Your skin tingles the way it does when you awake from a too-exciting dream and have to pace around the empty house wrapped in a blanket, waiting for the familiar creak of the floorboards to pull you back into an awareness of the ordinary, a regular relationship of your body and its world.*

"I'm ready to hear what you've come here to tell me," she says.

You haven't come to tell her anything, and say so, and then she is gone again, to collect herself, you suppose. Steve comes down from wherever he's been hiding out, and you're happy for that. You like Steve well enough, and in your calmest moments have even been jealous of the wholesome chapter he has entered into your mother's life.

"She'll be back in a few minutes," he says. "I was just going to make some coffee, if you'd like some."

"That would be lovely," you say, and he walks into the kitchen, speaking from there, though you do not follow him.

"Did you see your mother's new bushes on the way in?" he says, and you hear the clatter of ceramic mugs jostling together. "Azaleas or something. I'm sure she'd be thrilled if you mentioned it. We got your sister out here for a week last summer when they were only about ankle high, and she kept picking on your mom about how they looked. She was just joking, but you know how your mother is. I think she's feeling a little sensitive about the landscaping. They've filled out nicely though. Cream and sugar?"

"Both," you say. "Lots."

Affection has filled you up like a breath held underwater. He is just like her, of course, a nice life scaffolded with denials—but in her sensuality, she lacks his imagination. His little familial patter catches you at the ankles and sweeps you under, saying, "This is the life I have had; this is the family that has borne me." Untrue, maybe, but deep enough to swim.

"At least she can get them to grow," you say, and though your voice sounds fake and lilting, you think he hears and knows that you are trying. "She was always trying to make a garden at the old house, but the ground was too salty. She'd buy all these tomato plants and those little herb boxes. It killed her to watch them wilt."

"Well yeah," he says, "when a woman has a green thumb like your mother, she can't stand not to have some living things around her. Did you see the garden?"

You say you haven't, and he comes out of the kitchen grinning.

"Well come on then," he says, pressing a mug of coffee into your hands. "You're just in time for the last pumpkins."

A house has been constructed from your absence. Its architecture is that of her leaving. You can still remember the feeling of your house as she abandoned it—the way your noise echoed off the walls and the rooms felt so big with all her things taken out of them. That was in the days of the aftermath, in the new silence that came to replace the old one, the one that had been torn up and ruined in the fighting, the Fight.

Your father had been with you that morning. Mara was at school, but you were sick again. Your father was with you in your room, watching one of the cartoon movies he always rented from the grocery store when you had to stay home from school. You weren't really watching and do not remember what movie it was. Your mother had left an hour before, saying she was going to visit some woman from church and wouldn't be back until dinner. But she came back after only an hour. You didn't hear her car, so she must have parked down by the shed. She came into the room and stood by the door not saying anything. When she left, your father followed her down to the kitchen.

You do not know what it was that she saw. There is a lacuna in your memory of that day, smoothed over by a sense of the ordinary—whatever it was, it wasn't the first time, or the last. You cannot be sure. You cannot say for certain that it was not just a regular scene, another instance of his small and constant violence. Maybe you said something mouthy, and he hit you, hard with his open hand, leaving a swath of mottled red on your cheek. Perhaps she saw that one time too many. Maybe she saw him sitting home on a day when he should have been working, the bills piling up. Maybe she heard him call you a bitch, in the causal way he did to you then, and to Mara, and to her. You think this because you do not want to think, even now in your hatred of her, that she could have seen him there, with his fingers snaking up under your nightgown and the blankets pushed into a hillock above your small torso, and have seen in that only a getaway, only an opening door. It was near the beginning; she could have spared you years.

In the garden, the dirt gives up water around your feet, like grapes being pressed for wine. You had forgotten the softness of the inland air; stripped of its acerbity it is air only. You could be breathing in nothing, and it would catch you if you fell. The garden is less picturesque than you had hoped—just a rectangle of bare, dark soil, littered with the dried vines of the summer's harvest and a few floundering basils. A single behemoth pumpkin stands at the far end, slowly tipping onto the grass. *Your mother used to keep a picture of a cottage garden clipped from some ancient homemaker's magazine on her bedside table with her reading glasses and earring dish. You can easily recall the contours of the low stone wall that surrounded that much-loved picture-garden, and the branching arms of the small tree that stood behind it, casting shadows onto some ground-hugging greenery—maybe strawberries.*

"She planted some of everything this year, just to see what would make it. This was our big success of course," he says, rapping on the pumpkin with his knuckles. "Not quite county-fair material, but not bad for a first attempt."

A small, black cat, evidently disturbed by the noise, appears from behind the pumpkin and wanders towards you in an ambling, bad-tempered way. The fur on his head is flecked with gray, and he has the thin, sway-backed look of an animal artificially preserved. It takes you a half-second longer than it should to recognize him.

"Oh Abbot," you say, gathering his hissing, squirming form into your arms and pressing his face to yours, "Abbot you got so old."

"Oh yeah, he's out here all the time," Steve says. "I guess the dirt gets warmer than the grass."

He reaches out a hand to scratch Abbot's ears, but lets it drop without touching, as if to acknowledge your special claim. You nuzzle your face closer into thin, dandruff-spotted fur, afraid that Steve will see that you want to cry, though you will not.

"Poor old man," Steve said. "Mara wanted to take him when she moved, but your mother wouldn't hear of it. She said he's smelly and toothless, but he'll always have a home with us, just like you girls. He's been in the family almost as long as you two, anyway."

He's outlasted you, you think, but say, "We got him on Mara's fifth birthday."

Actually, you'd each gotten a kitten, but yours, Amber, had run off when she was only a few months old. She had turned feral out on the rocks. For years you would sometimes see her, or think you did, when you went out walking along the old pylon trail. She was a red tabby and had yellow eyes that you could see from anywhere. Your father had promised to get you a new cat, but you'd said you didn't want one. You'd forgotten that Abbot belonged to Mara until they took him with them when they went.

"I'm sure he's happier here. He's a West-Coast cat," you say. Abbot squirms again, and you set him down. Hundreds of dark hairs have attached themselves to your sweater, and you begin the long labor of picking them off.

"A coastal cat, really. He's the only cat I ever met that didn't hate water."

That's your fault; you tried to teach him to swim. He does hate water, but he accepts it as inevitable.

You nod, watching as Abbot totters, then sits, breathing hard. You should have been more careful with him.

[27]

"How were things up there?" Steve says to your silence. "Your mother mentioned that your landlord..."

"I'm leaving," you say, and it feels like a dam breaking to tell someone, and to realize that you've already left. "I'm going to Kansas to get married."

There are questions to be asked, and he settles on "why Kansas?"

"It's in the middle," you say. "The exact middle, actually. It's a little town called Lebanon, and it's the geographical center of the U.S. It seemed symbolic, I guess. It seemed fair. It won't be easy for either of us to go home."

"What's your father say?"

You think maybe you should be offended by this question, but there is a strange something in his tone, like commiseration or intimation, and so you let it go.

"I don't intend for him to know. He hasn't been living at the house for a while now. I asked him to leave right after I came back from Pennsylvania."

He's looking at you inquisitively, and you realize how little of your life they've known about, how it has reached them in rumors and reports.

"No one knew I was going to leave except Johnny," you say, "my boyfriend."

"Fiancée," he says, and you nod.

"There's no way Dad could find me."

"Your mother," he says, and you cut him off, not knowing or caring what he might say about her.

"I won't tell either of you how to reach me."

You wish this did not sound angry, but it does. You would like to tell him this is a purely tactical measure; if they knew, they would be required to tell by the terms of their arrangement with the past. They must tell or admit there is a reason not to. They would tell, and you can spare them that.

He is looking at the ground with an intensity that should churn the soil. His look could pull seeds from the ground, could sprout flowers from the place where his eyes will not meet yours. You want to turn away, but he is not even looking at you, so what is there to turn away from? You have always liked this man and have never guessed he knows as much as he seems on the verge of telling. You want to turn away from that too, and maybe he sees that because when he looks up he does not tell you what he knows.

"I'll let you work that out with your mother," he says.

The honesty has gone out of his eyes like the air out of a balloon—a comical show, the little piece of rubber swirling mad-cap through the air, pushed by the force of a bellowing, hilarious fart.

"Yeah," you say. "Sure. We'll work it out."

It would be a long while before you realized the importance of the fight they had that day—when she came home early and caught him at whatever she'd meant to catch him at—and by then you had forgotten the words they said. You are certain she threatened to leave; she did that often and with an obvious, if frustrated, sincerity. Did she say she would take you with her? You are sure you heard her say it, sometime, if not then. You were lying in your bed, and the movie was still playing, pale against the sun-lit curtains. It was the crucial moment. She said she'd take the girls, and he said that if she did... some threat, something that scared her. Something about you? Was that when the deal was made?

You have never, in all your long interrogations of this moment, been able to imagine what he might have said to her. That sentence—the incantation, the fatal announcement, the something—formed a gulf by which all things were divided: this side or that. They were, you think, the last words your parents ever said to each other. Two days later, your mother and sister were gone. The sound of their absence reverberated in those unheard words. Or, not the words—they were inaudible, unreadable, uninterpretable—but in the sound of the words' impact, the awful quietness by which you knew the decision had been made.

The fight had stopped so suddenly that you flinched. They had reached a final silence, and the house was calm; you could hear the curtains moving against the wood of the windowsill. The forgotten voices of your cartoon-movie characters clanged discordant and ugly, and you wanted to cover your ears. The years have interfered with your memory, and now you imagine that you can see your mother's face, can almost feel the ridges on her forehead forming as she is folded under the weight of realization, or horror, or jealousy, or the sudden, sky-opening possibility of freedom. You imagine the slump of her shoulders, the loss of breath, the shivering of her thin fingers as she realized that she would live a life beyond him. Until that moment, she must have believed that he would kill her someday, and, being trapped, she built herself a romance within the constraint. She was the glimmering object of a perverse and sorry love. She must have felt jilted, then, in some sad, small part of herself, to discover her deposition. She must have felt younger than she'd ever been because she had never been free of his desires of her. As always, she need only give him what he wanted, and then she could go. Her lacquered fingers gripped the edge of the sink, the noise of their quivering not breaking the deeper quiet in which she now could, and would, leave you.

Later she'd come into your bedroom and turned off the movie. It had finished, and you had rewound, thinking you would really watch it this time. She turned it off and told you that she and Mara were going on a trip that you couldn't come on because your daddy wanted you to stay. You were too old not to know that something awful was happening. But you were sick to your stomach and hadn't eaten all day, and you felt sweaty and cold all at once, so you didn't try to make her explain it or admit it. You acted as if you didn't know anything about it so that she would come and sit on the bed and put her hand on your forehead and purse her lips with a look like she was trying to feel for something underneath the stove. Her hand was cool and dry and felt good on your skin. You too knew something about making a trade.

By dinner time, your mother has re-emerged, now adorned in her full, loving-parent regalia. She has changed into one of those little, light-colored cardigans with the embroidered flower on the shoulder—the kind that mothers always seem to have but which you have never seen on the rack in any store, anywhere. She insists on taking you out for a "nice, warm meal," pronouncing it as if it is some sort of specialty of hers, as if you haven't had one in years. You remind yourself that you have come, first and foremost, to suck the milk of her guilt, and so you go and order twice as much as you can eat, and then dessert, ignoring the stares of the waiters who appear to be trading notes on you, astounded by the openness of your gluttony.

At home, your mother claims to be half-asleep from the vanilla martinis she had for dessert. She giggles as if she's said something naughty, though you only remember one martini, and she'd made Steve drink part of that. He'd looked embarrassed and grimaced at the taste, saying it was like liquid diabetic shock. You think he just wanted to look manly because his wife was doing her little-girl act, and this was the only way he got to play along. Still, you tell her she should go to bed and that you'll see her in the morning, and she rattles off a too-long list of things you ought to see while they have you. She is leaning in the doorway of their bedroom as Steve arranges Mara's old room for you. Just like old times. You can almost see the words forming in the shadows that swim across her eyes.

You think of Pauline, and of the letter-as-talisman you carried away from the place she'd stayed—stayed and stuck and never been uprooted. You feel a clench of horror at that, but see the ethic in it too. What would it have been, to keep your place? In the painting above the desk, her wide, accepting face had turned to look at you and everything around you, like a woman who had never meant to flee, who had never imagined the better world beyond her brief and vanishing life. Lying in the dark after your mother has closed the door, you wonder how long you will be expected to stay.

You'd come to your mother before, when you were sixteen, the one time you managed to run away. The sting of her abandonment had been fresher then, and you were younger, and you were very angry. Still, you went to her because you needed a place to go to, and because you once had loved her so desperately that you still felt a longing that seemed unnatural, outside of yourself. And your sister was there, and you felt you could run to her too, though she was still only a little girl.

You skipped school and snuck out of the house while he was working. (Working. You realize now it must have been a lie, and you wonder what it was then.) You didn't know her address or phone number, but you knew the name of the place and were such a small-town child that you assumed everyone would know her, would know all about you, would take you right to her door. There was a boy in your class who liked you—big-muscled and dissatisfied, a hulk, unconscionably angry and sure that everything he said was continually and willfully misconstrued. He thought you were "different" and told you one lunch break, when he had conspired to get you alone on the quad, that he wanted to run away with you. You let him drive you to the bus station and buy your ticket but somehow kept him from coming along. You don't remember ever seeing him after you got back, or even noticing his absence. You feel badly for this now. When you first met Johnny, you thought of this boy for the first time since the image of his blue 82' Chevy vanished from the Greyhound's window. You weren't looking, even then.

In Mt. Shasta, it had taken what felt like forever to track her down. No one knew her. She wasn't even in the phone book. You slept in the library during the day and sat up all night at the Denny's, slowly rationing out the money you'd taken from his wallet on hash browns and ice cream. When a librarian threatened to report you to the truancy officers, you finally got the idea that you should have had all along. Your mother had kept herself well hidden, but Mara was easy to find. You knew there would only be one at the Mt. Shasta Junior High, even though the last name was wrong. They brought her into the office from civics class, and she looked terrified when she came in, shaking and pale at just the idea of being in trouble, at having been called out, "like some sort of criminal," she'd later say, in front of everyone. In the fractional second before the hugging and the squealed hellos, before she buried her still-a-half-foot-shorter form in your baggy, dirty clothes and wouldn't let go, you think you saw a look pass over her face that you could not identify: you think you saw her shake harder.

Your mother came and picked you both up. She stood beside her little red Honda, wondering aloud if the post office would already be closed, and held the broken trunk open as you both tossed in your backpacks—as if the three of you were inhabiting a moment hundreds of miles away and years before. All through the ride, you waited for her to talk to you as her eyes appeared and disappeared from the rearview mirror, examining you, or perhaps just checking if the farm pick up behind had backed sufficiently away from her bumper. She said nothing, or nothing that mattered. You stopped at the post office and found it open.

[31]

At home, she gave you the "Grand Tour" before disappearing into the kitchen to cook, suggesting that you might want a shower. She took a fresh towel out of the dryer for you. As soon as you turned the water on, Mara knocked on the door and asked to come in. She sat on the sink and asked you questions. She had grown taller and thinner since you'd seen her last and had straightened her curly hair into long, highlighted waves. When she talked, she was straightforward, conspiratorial, and giddy—none of the childlike wandering that had characterized her for so long, supporting the family jokes about her air headedness. You could still see the occasional flash of braces, as much as she tried to keep her lips edged down around them. She was stranger to you than you were to her. She seemed not to realize how totally she had been transformed in the three years of her diaspora. She remembered you. You had not changed. You loved her familiarity, even if you could not share in it. Still, you didn't like the way it felt to have her look at you through the thin layer of steam gathering on the shower door, and you asked her to leave before you stepped out.

There was some trouble in finding clean clothes for you to wear—your mother's and sister's were too small—but you were finally outfitted in a t-shirt of Steve's that hung like a mini-dress and your mother's long-forgotten maternity jeans. She washed the clothes you'd brought with you and promised to take you to the mall the next day. Then there was dinner, with Steve telling a story about a man he worked with and stopping every so often to explain the details to you, but not so often that it made you feel strange. They made a bed for you on the couch, and from there you could hear them talking in their room for a little while, but you didn't know what they said.

You thought maybe Mara would come and talk to you again, but she did not. The two of you had shared a bedroom until you were ten and she was seven. At first, she'd been excited to have her own room, to be granted that little piece of grown-up status, but she soon discovered that she was afraid to be alone at night. She would wake up in darkness and get scared of the quiet and the loneliness. She would come into your room and stand in the doorway, shifting her weight back and forth on the creaky board. After a week, you got ugly with her, and she started going to your parents' room instead. A week after that they bought her an old, thirteen-inch TV because they'd decided that all she needed was to hear a human voice among all the old-house clattering and the sea-noises, and it didn't matter if it was yours or theirs or some actor's from the reruns. It worked, and, for years, the sound of Mara sleeping was the over-awed squeals of the infomercial women and the too-early chirp of the morning news. She'd taken the TV with her when she left, though it was so old by then that the images were like bodies pushing out from behind a curtain of snow. You realized you were listening for it, even then, to know that she was sleeping and would not disturb you. Perhaps you'd never stopped listening and hadn't slept in years, always waiting for the sound of footsteps at the doorway. Then your body felt too heavy—crushing, suffocating—and you wanted to hear a human voice.

You spent a few minutes searching for the remote to the living-room widescreen, pushing silently through the thick air of the sleeping not-your-house. When you found it, you turned the volume down until the actors were all whispering water-sounds to one another. Almost instantly, you were asleep.

Your mother woke you early with a hand on your shoulder.

"I knew I'd wake you anyway, rustling around," she said.

It was early. You sat for a long time, feeling the crimps and weak spots in your body, stretching them, trying to focus your eyes. Your mother had gone into the kitchen, and was, indeed, rustling around—making breakfast, you presumed. No one else was awake. After a while, she called you in and gave you a bowl of apples to peel.

"After brunch, I'm going to drop you and Mara off at the mall. One of her friends from school will be there, and I'm hoping you can chaperone them while I go for my run. After that I'd like if we could all have dinner somewhere nice, and then I'm afraid we're going to have to go back to the bus station."

In the moments before you exactly knew what was being done to you, your first instinct was to feel sorry for her—or worse, sorrow for her. She was standing with her back to you, chopping fruit into a large green bowl, and there was something terrible in the gesture, some willful attenuation poured through her tiny body. For that moment, you saw her structure—the hard scaffold that her soft and harried flesh covered, which she lived somehow within, doing these things. A chimera, an insect in its shell. Then that was gone, and there was only your useless screaming into her blank face.

On the bus that night, returning, you slept against the coldness of the window. In your jacket pocket were the ten twenties she had handed you along with your ticket. Whenever you awoke to a bump in the road, you would run the pads of your fingers along the bill's sharp edges, as if to scrape away the prints. You told yourself that as soon as the bus stopped you would get on another, that you would go anywhere. But when they left you off it was in the pre-dawn fog, and the station was a too-bright room where there were no people but only their leavings—muddy shoe prints and fast food receipts leaking ink into the floor. At the far end of the room was a locked door and a closed cashier's window with a sign saying, "Open at 6 am." Underneath the window was a little table with a coffeemaker left plugged in and a Styrofoam cup stuffed with sugar packets and powdered milk. Someone had written, "Help yourself" on a napkin, and you wanted to cry for the kindness of that. You drank some, though it was lukewarm and a spiral of something like egg whites slicked the surface.

You stood sipping it (straight back, above the tongue) and reading the schedules posted in the plastic case on the wall, and as you did the world compressed into a series of rooms like this one—an endless terrain of emptied-out almost-mornings, heavy-lidded and plastic-smelling: a bitter taste. This was the place that whispered to you in quiet, unpeopled moments, when you inhabited a world that seemed to have been built for your singular comfort. Perched in the stillness of that place, you could see the possibility of living through these rooms—of having and needing no more than they provided, of passing through them unseen and unprovable. You could have grown old in this feeling, could have stretched out into infinity, and scattered. It was the heart of the day, and you felt the awful tenderness of being a solitary creature, beloved of the world. It was not unbeautiful—years later you would remember the moment as a sort of revelation—but you were only sixteen, and the terrible loneliness of that vista left you gasping, overflowed with the child's terror of being left uncared for.

That you called him then, and that you let him come with the old truck through the gray of the dawn to take you home, was not evidence of your vacillation or uncertainty, nor of any wavering in your wish to escape him, but only of how much you were willing to trade in order to hear a human voice in that darkness.

5

In the morning, your mother decides that the two of you are going to go hiking. She wants to go to some mountain just outside of town; it is the same trail your mother and Steve took on their first date, and she hasn't been back there since, though it's just a short drive. "The time gets away from you," she says.

They'd met on some dating site where he'd described himself as an avid outdoorsman because he thought it would screen out the fat girls. He wasn't a slug or anything—he'd been an athlete in high school and for a while in college before his knees gave out—but it was a bit of a stretch. The ploy had worked well enough, and he'd met your mother and taken her hiking on their first date and basically never again. Now and again he'd join her for her runs and had even taken her camping for their anniversary one year, by some lake where they went out in a canoe and he let her reel in a few big bass. She tells you all this in the car, driving up the mountain roads a little too quickly, hands delicate and jittery on the wheel, and touching with only the middle third of her fingers, as if she is perpetually waiting for her nail-polish to dry.

She seems to want to talk about Steve a lot, in that cartoony, battle-of-the-sexes way women sometimes do when they are together in those de facto womanly places: behind the counter in diners, or the dressing rooms of department stores, in little-town social groups, or just anywhere they don't know each other too well. Maybe some women always talk this way—like they've all married these thick, stinking Neanderthals for some reason, and it is all just so funny. Big, hearty, feminine guffaws.

You guess she is going on like this because you let out over dinner that you are getting married when you get to Kansas. You said it because you thought she'd take it as a sign that you were settling into some sort of recognizable adulthood, and because you thought it would make her buy you things, but she just said, "I don't see a ring." You had to backtrack, saying that it wasn't really a formal thing, and you knew that sounded silly to her. "You're either engaged or you're not," she said, then the waiter came to clear your plates, and that had been the end of it. Now she was probably trying to make up for it, letting you into her weird, married-gal club.

You'd never wanted to get married—not for the thing itself. It was a means to an end, an escape route, the last train to salvation. You held onto the thought of Johnny for months after coming back from Pennsylvania, holding onto the sound of his voice on the phone as it echoed around the house you were alone in for the first time. You spoke loud

into the receiver, telling Johnny that your father was gone, that you'd made him leave,
and hadn't given in to his yelling and his threats. You did not tell Johnny that this new
strength had anything to do with him, that he was the hope you were sprouting. You did
not tell him, either, about the way that your father appeared on the porch one night,
tender and repentant with bags of groceries and a cheap but pretty necklace in a store-
wrapped box. Nor did you tell how you let your father come in and sleep on the couch,
and felt ashamed the next morning when you woke to find breakfast made for you and
him already gone. Ashamed for having let him stay, and for having locked your bedroom
door and lain awake most the night, terrified.

There would be time for telling Johnny that, you hoped. Instead, you told him that
you were lonely, and that you missed him and wanted him to stay with you the next time
he traveled west. You wanted him badly.

"This trail is really something special," your mother says, pulling onto
a dirt road marked by weathered Forest Service signs. "It's a bit steep for
the first part, but the view is worth it. You can see for miles. Last night I
was trying to think how I could show you all of town in such a little bit of
time, and then thought to myself, 'well, why not just get above it?'" She
laughs, and you laugh too because she is really trying to be so nice, and it
always makes you feel sick to your stomach when people hurt their
mothers' feelings, though you of all people should understand why that
might happen sometimes and be all right or even justified.

You park near the trailhead and get out. It does look like a pretty
place—big Douglas Firs hanging their branches over the road and casting a
cool, green shadow. The sound of water, or maybe just the feeling of it
heavy in the air.

"I'm surprised to see it so abandoned here on a weekend," your
mother says, leaning against the car and tightening the laces on her hiking
boots. You are wearing her old pair—just like her new pair, but she says
the arch supports aren't what they should be anymore. You would have
worn your big, red-leather work boots because you wear them for
everything, but she thought they were "too flat for the terrain," whatever
that meant. She is giving you these shoes, and you have to admit they feel
amazing—soft and pliable. You kept wanting to touch them on the ride
over and had kept your legs crossed uncomfortably at the knee so you
could. You can't imagine when you will ever wear them again.

"Everyone thinks it's going to rain, probably," she says, straightening
up. "We've got them fooled, though. Any money says it will hold off until
evening."

She looks up at the sky while she talks, but gives a sidelong smile now,
to see how this news has struck you. She's always been proud of her little
forecasts. They are meant to make her seem earthy and born of that place,

and usually she is right. She has brought two small backpacks stuffed with bottled water and little bags of trail mix—matching, pale green. You wonder why she bought them and what partner she'd imagined. She sets them on the hood of the car and begins stretching, her arms moving in slow, elegant arcs over her head, the motion punctuated at the outside edge by a little swing of the hip like a cha-cha dancer's. You think you should join, but your body feels heavy and awkward in her presence. She keeps her eyes closed, and her face becomes a serene blankness, an expanse. She has escaped into the private world that stretches out backwards from behind her eyelids. *You've always sensed it there; you have watched her going away and returning, a hundred times a day. Her favorite phrase when you and Mara were kids was "I'm crawling out of my skin." She'd say it as your father walked in the door. You'd pictured it literally and been both appalled and strangely excited. Like her, you do not like to be confined.*

"Well, off we go," she says, dropping her arms and opening her eyes, returning with an expression like someone looking over vacation photos or numbers on a paycheck: fulfilled. She turns and takes off up the trail as if she had forgotten you were there at all. You are a hundred feet behind at the end of the first minute.

"Mom," you say. "Mom, wait up."

She does, stopping to watch you as you walk, looking at you steadily the whole time. You look away then, but she looks happy. When you are side by side, she walks again, slower now, but with the same urgency— quick steps with her hands grasping the straps of her backpack, her eyes crisscrossing the trail ahead. *You had remembered her more languid. Perhaps she had been, then; there was a creeping quietude in the house where you'd grown up—in the land—a slowness that grew into the blood of its inhabitants, slowing to an inevitable drought. Or perhaps you are only confusing her with the woman you have become, recasting her in memory so many times that the paint has begun to wear away and she has been revealed as just another image of yourself.*

"I'm sorry," she says. "I'm just so used to walking on my own. Just let me know when you need a rest."

You swear to yourself that you will not ask for this accommodation from her—will not ask for anything, yet, at least—but soon the trail begins to rise precipitously, and you feel an unfamiliar ache in the backs of your thighs as you struggle to keep your breathing quiet. You do not want her to hear you gasp. You would like her to think you are strong. You would like for the life she chose to have made her weaker, at least.

"So tell me about this boyfriend," she says. You do not want to do this.

"Johnny. He's great," you say, and you mean to say more, you're just taking a moment to think, but she won't wait.

"Well, I should hope so. What does he do?"

It's such a snotty, middle-class thing to ask. You're sure of it now, she wasn't always like this.

"He's a jack-of-all-trades, I guess." The phrase sounds fake and antiquated, as if you've announced that you're marrying a milliner or an apothecary. You're speaking some ridiculous language you've made up on the spot to impress her—or the rich, judgmental woman you think she might now be. "He worked in a restaurant in Virginia until last week, but he's done just about everything at some point or another. He worked construction for a while, and he might do that again in Kansas. It's mostly farms there, though, and I think he's interested in that. He likes that sort of physical stuff."

"That's hard work," she says, even though these are just lies you are telling, extemporaneous imaginings. You haven't talked with Johnny about anything like that. For the first time, you feel a jolt of real, practical terror—the nearness of failure. "He'd do better to settle into something," she continues. "Something long term."

"He likes hard work," you say. "He'll do what he can do."

This isn't really the answer you would like to give, but your mind is already racing ahead to the other questions she is sure to ask. Where you will live and whom you will know and how sure are you of him or even of yourself who, at twenty-two, has done little beside work part-time in a grocery store and swim in the ocean and survive some injustices, which isn't much and doesn't prepare you for anything? *And you think you'd have a lot to say to those questions—a lot to say about how she was no different when she'd married your father, younger than you are now, because he was "brilliant" in a way that was obvious to everyone and never, ever borne out in his actions. And he'd jumped from job to job, and always jobs that were below him so that his bosses hated him for being superior and lazy, and he'd gotten angrier with every job he lost. And so they never had anything, but they had gone ahead and had you anyway, for reasons you could never even begin to understand, and then had Mara too, and raised you both in that falling-apart, rented house up on the bluff which you had only now, finally, had the strength to leave. And what had she ever done but leave? Leave and start something new somewhere else, so if she didn't want you to do that, what did she want you to do?* But she doesn't ask any of those questions. Instead, she walks a few paces ahead and smiles and says, "I hope you'll call," and your answers go stale in your mouth. You roll the ball of them under your tongue, try to swallow. It is an earth taste, a bitter taste, like vitamins. Perhaps she is on to you—knows that you hold the advantage against any criticisms she could make—or perhaps she really means well. Perhaps she trusts you.

"How's Mara?" you say, and you see her nod her head a few times before answering, like she's convincing herself of something, which means she's lying.

"She's good," she says. "Don't you two talk? I had gotten the impression you did, last time she was home."

"We do, some," you say. "It's been awhile."

She'd started calling you the spring after she left for college. The first time had been late—eleven or twelve, and your father had just gone to bed. From your chair in the hallway between your rooms, you could hear him breathing. When the phone rang, you jumped up with your heart pounding, sure it was bad news, though now you have no idea what news could have possibly disturbed you, in your little life, or who would have called.

"Jane, it's Mara," she said, "but don't say anything. If he's there just hang up. I'll call back, I promise."

"Hold on," you whispered, "just hold on." But aloud you'd said, "I'm sorry, I think you have the wrong number."

It took forever to get down the stairs, trying to move light and casual. You removed the kitchen phone from its hook without turning on the light, afraid that the glow would reach him through his window, a brightness on the lawn. You worried about this as you climbed back up the stairs to replace the hall phone and as you climbed down again. You were sure she'd be gone when you got back, and it all seemed so silly, anyway. He was just a bogeyman to her—it had all reduced so simply—and how much did she even remember? You played along because you did not want her to hang up, and you felt your pulse racing as you traced your figure eight across the house, as if you too were afraid.

"Mara?" you said. You had the receiver in one hand and clutched the cord with the other, as if it were a tether in the shifting waters of the room and the darkness. You tried to judge by the sound of your own words whether they were dropping into the strange emptiness of an abandoned line—listening for that sudden extinguishment—and you decided that they were. Then she said, "Hey," and you wondered what noise you had been listening for at all; where had you heard it before?

"I would have called sooner," she said. "I tried. I tried a few times, and you never picked up, but I should have called a long time ago."

"It's okay," you said. "Where are you?"

"I'm at home," she said. "In my room, I mean. I'm in school now. I'm a freshman at Muhlenberg College."

Her voice was lower and wetter than you remembered, and you thought she might have been drunk, or crying, but she sounded so proud when she said this that you felt something you took to be your heart pushing at the walls of your chest, as if it wanted to crawl out of you, across the phone lines, to her.

"Where is that?" you said, and when she answered, "Pennsylvania," you said, "Oh my God, Mara, that's so far," and had felt the distance between you like counting the seconds between a bolt of lightning and the thunderclap—the lengthening wait. It had been years since you'd seen her, but at least you'd always been able to imagine her a long bus-ride away, been able to remember the place she lived in, the feeling of her living there. You tried to imagine how she would look now, a college freshman in Pennsylvania, but you could not. Your memory contained only a fat-cheeked child who was at once Mara, and a little girl from a TV commercial, and a shifting blur that wasn't even a face at all.

"Far was kind of the point," she said. "I had to get away. I've never been anywhere."

You knew this was crazy because she'd always been somewhere else.

"And," she said, her voice becoming propped-up and grave, "I always felt like I couldn't call when I lived at home. Mom, you know, and... It wasn't even that. It just never crossed my mind that I could."

"It's okay," you said, "I never called either."

"I didn't expect you to. How could I?"

You were her older sister and did not know what she could mean by this, her voice gone soft and so very understanding.

"How's school?" you asked, and she laughed and didn't answer—laughed as if she didn't know you expected her to answer.

"You're okay?" she said.

"I'm fine," you said. Your voice came out a cold little snap, and you didn't realize until after you heard it that you were feeling annoyed. Prodded.

"What are you majoring in? Do you still like science? Bio?" You felt ridiculous saying this because what you were thinking of was salamander hunts in the garden and amorphous rubber-skinned creatures pulled out of tide-pools—the slime they sometimes left on your bare hands. Maybe she caught this in your voice because the next thing you heard was a sob, rending and singular. You were not, at first, able to name the sound of her crying; it seemed so full, so beyond her. For a moment, you were left contemplating the noise. It was shaped like a wave: first, a pulling in, a vacuum being filled and overfilled, a drowning gulp, and then a cresting and a crash that pulled her down into silence. Just one sob, quickly stifled. You stood in your kitchen, thousands of miles away from the unimaginable place where she was crying, and you said nothing because that was the only language you could be sure the two of you still shared.

"I'm sorry, Jane," she said then, her voice cleared so quickly you wondered if you had really even heard. "This is just a lot. I don't know what to say now. Mom never told me what he did to you until last year. I knew before that, I guess, but she'd never said it. I'm so sorry, Jane, but I didn't want to believe it, and I just tried not to know it. But I think about it all the time now. I just want you to have my number, and I want us to *talk. Not now, probably, but whenever you can. I want us to talk and figure some things out. This is so much all at once."*

"Okay," you said. She gave you her number and said that she loved you and that you should call her whenever you wanted, and then she was gone again.

You felt dull and slow and stood for a while, wrapping and unwrapping the slip of paper with her number scribbled on it around your index finger. You did not know what she had meant, or meant to do, and began to wish she had not called. You had imagined seeing her again, now and then over the years, sometimes wanting it badly. You had often thought that the worst part of what had happened in your family, the one truly unforgivable thing, had been the theft of your baby sister from you. But you had thought this in moments of righteous anger—had thought it about them and not about her. You wanted the feeling of having known her, which was different from missing her, which was its inverse. Finally you went to bed, leaving her number in a drawer of your desk, hidden under a pile of old magazines that you had once wanted to keep and now found it too much trouble to throw away.

In the morning, the whole thing seemed stranger, and the call had gotten wrapped up in the dreams it caused you. You awoke with a sudden understanding, as if she had spoken it right into you: to her you had become something other than yourself. You had become a frozen point, an endlessly recapitulated moment of crisis. For her, you were the rupture. It was unthinkable that you would have a life apart from your importance, and so she did not want to see you or know you so much as she wanted to mend you. You did not blame her, but you also did not call her for a long time—four months, almost.

"Well, Mara says she going to start taking classes again in the spring. I think she's getting fed up with those people she lives with. It doesn't sound like any of them have jobs," your mother says, talking up the trail instead of towards you.

"Does she?" you say, but she just looks at you, and you realize how rude you are, to talk about your mother's daughter that way.

In the months after Mara's call, you thought about her often, whenever you did something you knew she would not believe or accept. It became a game, to find yourself in these surprising places and to imagine it all as a scrawled-on, postcard picture: "Dear Mara, I sure do get around for a ghost and a problem. Love, Jane."

You defined widely the things Mara would not believe you could do. Some days it seemed that just getting out of the house qualified, just driving to work on time and being happy enough there, separating the meat from the laundry detergent and helping the older ladies carry their bags to their cars, even though they said they'd make it on their own. Sometimes it was when you'd take smoke breaks with Jeannie or Alex or one of the other girls, and they'd talk about their boyfriends, and sometimes they'd invite you to see a movie on the weekends or to go get drinks at the tourist bars in Lincoln City where they had three-dollar margaritas, and sometimes you'd go.

You certainly thought of Mara on those nights when you did go out with Jeannie and Alex, and they'd run into some guy they knew, some friend of their boyfriends' or someone's cousin, and you and this guy would end up dancing, fast and close so you felt like everyone was watching. Sometimes you'd end the night making out in the back booth where everyone on the way to the bathroom had to walk right past, and sometimes you did go home with these guys and fuck them in their apartments where everything sat on the floor—the mattresses and the TVs and the boxes of pictures and books. For the most part, though, you did not, and instead Jeannie would drive you home and say, "It looks like you had fun," with a big goofy smile, as if there was some secret detail you might still have to reveal.

Mostly though, you thought about Mara on Thursday nights when you and your dad would drive into town to go to O'Malley's. You'd done this every week from the time you were eighteen. It was one of those fake-Irish sports bars that have shamrock decorations on the walls and dark wood everywhere and insist on appending the word "pub" to half of their menu items. Really, though, it was just like any other bar except that their burgers were half-priced on Thursday nights until nine, and after a while, you got to know the waitresses. You'd go in at eight and each order a beer, which was the appeal for you at first, because no one would ever check your i.d. when you were with your dad. If the waitress was new and did ask, you'd just make a big show of digging through your purse until your dad said, "She was born in 1985, if that's what you need to know. December 18th. It was pouring down hail like a mother-fucker and I said, 'Janie, couldn't you just wait a day?'"

Actually, you had waited five years, but you'd just smile and keep digging, and the waitress would say, "Oh, don't worry about it," and bring out your beers in those big Guinness pint glasses, though you didn't drink that. You'd tried everything they had on tap and found it didn't make much difference to you, so mostly you just drank Rainier because it was cheapest, and your dad drank Newcastle because he said it was "the best value," and, you guessed, because he thought that his drink should always be darker than his daughter's. After a while, you would each order a big, oozy burger with some weird name you always refused to use when ordering, just pointing at the description instead. As you handed your menus back, your dad would usually say, "Those are on special, right?" though he must have known they were, and the waitress would say, "Until nine," and you wondered, sometimes, if he was even aware of asking.

You both ate in the same way—too fast, in ambitious, greasy-lipped gulps that you'd always try to talk through before they were quite swallowed, tearing hunks off the top of your bun to sop up the drippings of fat and cheese. Sometimes you would swap ingredients—his extra tomatoes for your dill pickle—and sometimes you would just sit, spinning the ketchup bottle on the tabletop, talking about your weeks. Nothing ever really happened, but there were enough things to say. You both went to jobs and fought

with bosses, though sometimes he got fired, and you never did, and there was always the
house, with its innumerable quirks and his jury-rigged repairs. He'd explain every
problem he fixed in too much detail, using his hands to gesticulate on the table, big bear-
hands balanced on their fingertips, looking like two horrible spiders sprouting thick
black hair from their knees, their knuckles. Sometimes you'd get another beer, and
sometimes he would get two more, or three, and then the ride home would be bad—the
cab of the truck filling up with the substance of his quiet so that you would want to roll
the window down and stick your head out as far as it would go and hear the wind, at
least. But mostly you just had a beer and a burger apiece, drove home, and said
goodnight to each other in the hallway between your rooms.

Years later, when you told Johnny this, he said that you sounded like a person
with Stockholm syndrome, weeding out the real awfulness to display these insignificant
moments of contentment, identifying with your captor. Well sure, sure you thought, but
aren't all families like that? At least a little? So this is what you wanted Mara to
know, that the things that had happened in your family were catastrophes, but in
between the catastrophes had been years. It had been as solid and simple as years.

"She called yesterday, before you arrived," she goes on, her face
softening again. "She was worried because she'd heard something on the
news about floods up north of here."

"I thought the floods were on the coast. The road was blocked
yesterday," you say.

She shrugs.

"Maybe there too. It's been a rainy week all over. Didn't you run into
any of it on your drive?"

"Yes," you say, "but I didn't think it was so bad. I'm used to weather."

"Well, the ground's not," she says, "and that's what matters."

You look at your shoes and notice that they are caked with mud
halfway to your ankle. This, you tell yourself, is why you are so tired.

"The neighbors down the road have had water over their threshold
twice this week," she says, "but we've been lucky. We've never flooded,
even though we're in a valley."

"That's weird," you say, but she just smiles, as if it were something
she'd done herself, as if she'd stopped the water at the door.

"It did in my lilies, though. Yesterday morning I found them out on
the lawn. The bulbs had washed right out of the ground."

"That's too bad," you say, and she gives three sharp little nods.

Then there was a Thursday night four months after she called. This was in June,
and the air was so beautiful—as wet and heavy as steam—and you couldn't take a step

into the yard without disrupting a settlement of grasshoppers. They'd erupt out of the grass with each footfall, spindle-legs creaking, and the world felt very alive. Your dad had come home sullen and dreamy from a day you could not reconstruct. He was supposed to be working for some guy he'd met at the American Legion who owned a landscaping business, but the jobs kept getting canceled due to rain. This seemed strange to you since it rained all the time there by the coast, and if they couldn't landscape in the rain you didn't know how they could landscape at all. You considered the possibility that there were things you were not being told.

Still, he'd been up and gone before you awoke, and when he came back, late in the afternoon, he'd seemed tired and broken-down and had only stood for a moment in the kitchen, looking past you to the liquor cabinet, or maybe just out the window to the water. You'd asked him what was the matter, but he had not answered, had only pulled his jacket back on and stalked off to the shed where he was always working on some project or another. You'd liked to go in there when you were little—not while he was working, but after—to examine the oddly-shaped scraps of wood fallen beneath the circular saw, or to try your arms against the tightly-screwed mason jars which stood in the window sills, jealously guarding a secret collection of odd-sized screws and unmatched door hinges. Now it had been years since you'd stepped foot in that room, except to peer over his shoulder at the ever-growing disarray as you told him that there was food on the stove for him, or that you were going out and not to wait up. Likewise, he had not been in your room for a long time—for nearly as long.

He came back into the house as the sun was setting and found you reading in the upstairs hall. He tossed your jacket onto your lap and said, "Ready?" and you said, "Sure," but you felt sleepy and heavy, and the bulk of him there, blocking your light, bothered you.

"Well what the fuck you waiting for then?" he said. He was looking into the floor when he said this, and his voice sounded forced by something that was not anger. The question sounded rhetorical, or perhaps simply insane. He was shifting his weight back and forth on his feet and running his hand through his hair fast, almost scratching: the familiar gestures of his dis-ease. You felt a cold pain in your throat, sliding down into your stomach like an ice cube, too large and unchewed.

There had been a slow, quiet period when he was diligent about working or looking for work and had let you do as you wished more or less without comment. On the first of each month, he had given you half the rent money, and a few hundred more for the groceries. On Saturdays, he would stay in half the morning, fixing whatever had broken during the week. He was not often angry—not, at least, at you. He had become a sort of helpmate, a sort of companion.

There was a tabulation you kept in your head, a running tally. You do not know how long you kept these records—you are not, otherwise, good with dates. Your memory is weak, and you forget birthdays, sometimes faces. The knowledge you retain, you think, must be of a different sort—instinctual, a circadian rhythm. You knew then, without thought, as you sat watching his face twitch between confusion and anger, remorse and pain, that it had been six months since he'd missed a payment on the rent or the utilities, eight since he had borrowed your money without telling you why, a year since he had stolen it. It was three months since he had gotten too drunk in public and made a fool of you, calling you names in front of all those people at the bar. It was six years since he had gotten in a fistfight. It was six years since he had been arrested. It was ten weeks since he'd been on unemployment and almost seven months since he had been fired from a job rather than "let go." It was a year and a half since he had said anything cruel enough to make you cry. It had been three years since he had hit you. In a month, it would be five years since he had touched you, or made you touch him.

But now, as he stood impatient and tight-wound in front of your chair, demanding of you as always, you imagined the tallies turning one by one. And on the translucent curtain that your mind's eye kept strung between you and him: a shimmering row of zeroes.

You stood, and the movement of your arms as you pulled them into your jacket sleeves seemed to push the curtain away—to break him, momentarily, from the coil of tension he was compressing into. He turned, and you followed him down the stairs wordlessly, out into the dropping dusk. You paused on the porch, liking the feeling of the cool, damp air. You sat on the porch swing, and he went on to the truck, which always sat down at the far end of the driveway because he said he didn't want anyone to be able to see from the road whether he was home or not.

Since you were small, no one ever walked that last hundred yards with him. His passengers always waited on the porch while he got in and turned the truck around. Sometimes there would be mud and the sound of the tires sinking and spluttering, but he always made it without help. When you were young, you remember him sometimes saying to you, "No reason to waste your steps" as he held out his hand, pointed up from where he stood on the flagstones: a gesture that meant, "Stop there." Now he no longer said this, but sometimes you still found yourself imagining that you only had so many steps allotted to you, and that you might someday find that you had used them up—somehow, stupidly, a case of poor accounting.

You have never known why he would not let you walk to the truck with him, what secret played out on that short trip behind the shed and away down towards the bluff. Amongst the catalogue of solitary moments he demanded from you each day, why this one more? You thought once that perhaps the essential part of his solitary driveway walk was not the time after he was disappeared from sight at all, but the moment of his walking away with you still there, watching. You thought he wanted to be admired. You had never been able to un-think this, once the idea was formed, though you are not sure that you really believed it to be true. He was, in a way, handsome. Handsome in the sense you might say an animal is handsome—broad and heavy, a body built to work and to withstand. Nothing extra, no prettiness or refinement, no fripperies. He was noble in that way, in the way he walked with his back straight and his feet lifting only just

[45]

enough, the stride long though he was short. This, you supposed, was something he might have wanted you to see, to force you to see. He was proud in his body.

You watched him that night as all other nights, noticing, despite yourself, the firm course of his arms—you couldn't call it a swing. After he was gone, you sat for a long while, tense and marooned there in the island of the porch-light as it grew slowly more defined against the curved edge of the darkness. You did not hear the sound of the engine—the drowsy whirring of half-worn parts pulled from junkyards and garage sales. The sound of the truck making its rattling way down the drive had become, for you, the palimpsest of all decay. Perhaps if you had known your grandparents you would have thought of them instead, on those mornings when you awoke sore and cold-muscled from swimming, or dancing, or elsewise. Maybe then the popping of their bones would have been the echo you heard in your own as you eased over onto your hip and swung your feet towards the floor. As it was, they were dead or gone before they could leave any impression on you, even of their loss, and so the sound all mortalities made was the truck's deep-voiced, oil-leak clatter. So you sat still and quiet on the porch swing, hoping to hear that sound; you feared the day the truck would not start as the acute downward turn in a progression of diminishing resources.

So when, instead of the truck, you heard his footsteps on the gravel, coming back towards you, you stood and rushed to the edge of the light, almost beyond, pushing forward to see what was on his face.

"It's dead?" you said, when he was close enough. It was a question, but you made sure to drop your voice down low at the end—a solemn statement. "Just the battery? Or the starter this time?"

"The truck's fine," he said. He walked past you and took the place you had emptied on the swing. He sat with his legs stretched out in front of him, rocking forward and back with his heels planted firmly on the wood of the porch floor. "I just thought maybe we could give it a miss tonight."

"Yeah?" you said, staying at the bottom of the steps. "Why's that?"

"Come up here, Janie," he said, patting the place beside him on the swing. "There are some things I want to talk about."

"I'm fine here," you said. "Let's just go." You were tensing for a fight. You could feel your blood in your skin.

"Don't be this way," he said.

"I'm not being any way," you said, lying.

"You're being that bitchy way you get. Now just come up here, I just want to talk about something. Can you do that for an old man? So your poor old father doesn't have to shout."

Even a few years before, you would have told him he wasn't shouting, and then, soon, he would have been, and it would go on and on. But now it was like you could watch it all play out in your mind, the whole scene, and there was no point to it no

[46]

matter what you did, and so you went, sitting beside him on the too-small swing, the sides of your thighs pressed against his, though you turned your face away.

You thought he would say something, but he didn't. You sat beside one another, looking down to the bluff or over across the road, and you watched as the dusk settled into dark. You heard these noises: waves, crickets chirping and rustling on the ground, his breathing—a little phlegmy—the wind hitting the rocks of the bluff and changing course, the wind tugging at the roof shingles, the creak of the porch swing's chains, your own breathing, and traffic, far away. You had imagined, in the first few moments of this sitting, several variations on the thing he wanted to tell you—the certainly bad thing he would, eventually, tell you. Now that seemed to matter less, or to matter only in the way that a storm matters as you watch it move in across the water, after the hatches are battened down, and there is only that strange ozone wind and the greening sky to tell you that you are waiting for something.

Then he began to talk, all of a sudden, as if there had been no pause at all.

"You're a good girl, Jane," he said, patting your thigh with his near hand, patting three times as he spoke, three heavy hand-falls. "I'm sorry about all of this."

"All of what?" you said, keeping your voice impartial and soft, but not so soft that he could get around it. You hung it out there in front of you—a wall, nothing more. He was good at evasions. He would confess, mourn, and repent without ever naming the thing he'd done.

"I never was good at guessing how things would turn out. And now I've just been waiting all this time, just waiting for something to come along without planning for what would happen if it didn't."

"I don't know what you mean, Dad. What's wrong? Right now, what's wrong?"

He was turning heavy-faced and wet-voiced, and you'd never get it out of him if you let him go on this way.

"I know what you think, Janie. You think I've just been doing what's best for me all these years, not thinking about what responsibilities I have to you. I understand why it would seem that way. I swear, Janie, sometimes I think of when your mother and I first had you, of how little and helpless you were, and I promise I wanted to give you more than this. I just didn't know how, baby-girl. I just never learned how."

The wind was picking up, or perhaps just becoming colder, as it always did in the night, but as you said, "I've had a good life, Dad. I know you've done your best for me," you wished he would let you move inside. He seemed to like the sting of the cold, though—to want it.

"I've never deserved a girl like you," he said.

He sighed, big and jagged, as if he really needed the air—as if the air were a glass of water, and he was thirsty.

"I don't have that landscaping job anymore. I lost it last week."

"I wish you would have told me," you said, dropping your eyes to the ground, trying to keep your body very still.

[47]

"I'm telling you now because I thought I could fix it. I don't worry you when I don't have to. You don't even know how many things I've dealt with—big things—that I never told you about because I didn't want you to worry."

"I didn't know that, like you said. I'm sorry. What happened with the job?"

"That fucking jackass Dan Maynard. I told him when he hired me that I didn't have experience. He said he'd train me, but that was bullshit. They had me working on my own the first day, and I figured it out fast too. I'm not trying to make excuses, Jane. By the third day, I was as good as anyone on that team. His own foreman said so."

"So what happened?" You too love the sound of your voice when you say this: so practical and so kind.

"The bastard had just hired too many people. Then the rain, and he wasn't making enough. He could of just been straight about it, he could of laid me off so I could at least get unemployment from it, but he made up some shit about me breaking a piece of equipment instead. Made it my fault. The man was a fucking crook, Janie."

"Why wouldn't he want you to get unemployment if you hadn't done anything wrong?"

"That's what crooks do."

"I'm sorry," you said, "but it will be all right. We're still up a couple of paychecks."

He shook his head slowly, back and forth until the movement seemed to blur into unconsciousness. He kept shaking his head this way, even as he spoke.

"He said I had to pay for the machine I broke. I didn't break it neither, but he's got records that say I was the last one working it. Fucker said he'd take me to court if I didn't pay. You remember the last time we went to court, Jane. I'm still paying that goddamned lawyer, and for what? So I told him to just keep what I'd made and be done with it, but he says I still owe him. I just spit right on his fucking desk and walked out when he said that, and I haven't heard from any fucking lawyer since. I'd bet the bank now he didn't have shit to back him up. I knew the records were bullshit, but what was I supposed to do? That kind of job makes it so a man can't stand up for himself. You don't get any kind of respect when you're working for a crooked bastard like that. Not from anyone. It just burns me up. I should have shoved his fat face into the goddamned floor."

"I wouldn't have blamed you if you did," you said.

He leaned back in the swing and sighed again.

"Yes you would of. A man can't always act like a man when he's got a family to think for. You're the only thing that's kept me honest all these years. Probably the only thing that's kept me from doing something crazy. And I just can't stand it sometimes, to think of how bad I always fail you."

He was pulling his hand back and forth across his face, the skin around his eyes stretching grotesquely, revealing red, and the white curve of the eyeball. When he rested his face in his palm then, you did not believe he was crying, but you were not sure.

You remember once or twice when you were very young, coming home from kindergarten to find your mother crying because, she said, your father had told her a lie, and telling lies would always hurt the people you told them to. Now you found it wasn't his lies that bothered you but his half-truths, the things he managed to make himself believe. These confounded you, these you found yourself worrying over nights, trying to make some firm divider between the things that were and the things he said. You thought if it were not for you, he would have lived a filthier, more tenable life.

So that was all of it then, just another lost job, another avoidable disaster that would mean you picking up double shifts and selling childhood toys as "collector's items" on the internet. And there he was, squalling in shame, confessing as if it were the first time, emoting in performance of his penitence. All through it you'd played your role perfectly, calm and strong, with just the right hint of hurt to woo him, dropping your head to stare at the floor, and now you grew teary-eyed too, put your hand on his back saying, "It's fine, it's all right. You did nothing wrong. You tried your best. All right, it's all right, all right." An ecstasy of forgiveness. You forgave everything in a glut of weeping. He loved for you to forgive him. You'd done it a thousand times.

Afterwards, you always wondered if he believed in these little shows he orchestrated. Does the trainer, giving his secret signals, really believe he's taught the horse to count? The secret signal: when he began speaking, when he said, "You're a good girl, Jane," and dropped his hand onto your thigh, it had stayed there, planted and clay-heavy, an ugly little animal you were afraid to wake. It lay straight across your leg, the palm planted on top, halfway between knee and crotch, and the fingers stretched around, their tips brushing the inside seam of your jeans: a hard line, a Rubicon that they slowly crossed. In your head your tallies were dissolving, melting beyond zero and into the muck of years, and you kept thinking, "I'm twenty-one years old," because it was the only way you could think to put a shell around the moment, to keep it from washing into the sea of the way it always was. And then, within the confines of those minutes when his hand was touching you—pulsing now and again, a little spasm in the muscles reminding you of how things had been worse and could always be worse—he asked you for something, and yes, of course, you gave it to him.

Once you had forgiven him, and once his hand had gone away, leaving a warmth and a small dampness, he asked you if you still wanted to go out, but you said you weren't really hungry anyway, and maybe you should just try to save your money. He said all right and went into the kitchen to make himself dinner, and you sat yourself in front of the TV in the next room, wrapped in a blanket and waiting through the hours until he went to bed. Then, after he came in and tousled your hair like he used sometimes to do when he was especially pleased with you, and after he climbed the stairs, and you heard his door close, scraping against the floor, swollen by the humidity, the recent rains, then you got up and went into the kitchen to pick at the leftovers of his meal—a bit of roasted chicken, a few stale rolls, a Budweiser. You were starving, and you scraped your teeth along the bones, searching out with your tongue the crevices where the meat still hung. Then, when you were finished and had wiped the grease from your hands, you picked the phone up from its hook and called Mara. You remembered the number.

Around you the trees are thinning out, bare branches reaching into the empty spaces left by leaves and the broken trunks that hang at strange angles—widow makers, you've heard them called—clutching giants' handfuls of dirt in their exposed roots. You do not know what could have caused this up-heave—wind, maybe, or water. The damage looks fresh— green wood and black dirt. You walk for a long while and notice the air getting colder. You try to keep your breathing shallow because there is a wet-chill ache forming in your chest that wraps itself up through your jaw and into your front teeth.

"How far do you think we've gone?" you ask, trying to sound merely curious.

"It's another mile," she says, "but there's a closer look-out, which I think is better anyway. You don't see as far, but it's more scenic. We'll turn off there," she says, pointing to a bent path cutting through the underbrush a few yards ahead. It looks overgrown and neglected, but heads, at least, downhill.

"Shortcut," she says, stepping off the trail and pushing her way through blueberry bushes and heavy, nameless undergrowth that seems halfway to bolting and halfway decayed. You walk to where the paths intersect and turn, picking your way over rocks and slippery masses of dead leaves which release a strange, mushroomy scent under your feet. Saltless, you realize, after you've crushed a few. Your mother steps onto the path behind you and walks close. Why doesn't she get in front? You feel her getting impatient with your mincing steps and your slow, branch-grabbing descent. You try to go faster, becoming afraid. The rocks are slick with mud.

"You're safer than you think," she says at last, and you've yelled at her before you know you mean to.

"You're such a liar," you say. "You're always such a liar."

She pushes ahead of you and hops down the rocks, bravely, long strides, showing off or just showing you how. You wrap both hands around a thick vine that hangs next to the trail, giving it your weight as if you were dangling from it over some great drop, afraid to let go. "My safety is the last thing you've ever cared about," you say to her back, watching to see it tense.

She stops on the trail ahead and stares back at you. You do not know what to say to her now. You had expected her to go on, straight ahead, not to stand there and look at you with a big-eyed, wounded face. She is trying

[50]

to think of something she can say that will deny the words you've just spoken, that will rope you back in to the comfortable world she has built to hold you. She cannot, and finally she just throws her hands above her head in a quick, frantic gesture, turns, and walks down the trail ahead of you. You follow because there is nothing else to be done.

Ahead of you, the trail ends in a little ledge and a sheer cliff. You stop short, twenty feet from the drop-off, afraid of this place. Your mother walks out to the ledge and then circles back, disappearing into the brush while you stand and stare out across the opening space. The wind blows up over the edge, so moist you think it will condense on the heat of your skin. Below is the bowl of the valley and the slow sweep of a higher mountain beyond, snow on its peak. You hear a sound that is like water—maybe a falls below?—but is also like bad weather moving in. You can see it there, the flashes of lightning across the valley, the line of rain like a curtain pulled down from the sky, except that it is also like a living thing, an animal bristling beneath its dark fur. The gray shale blends into the gray of the body of the rain, and you think for a wild, animistic moment that it means to trick you, to lead you out onto the air, which cannot hold your weight.

You are thinking now of the cliffs behind the Big Lots back home—a weird empty place that should have been worth something but wasn't because of the strip-mall traffic and the paved no man's land of dumpsters and loading docks that infringed upon it. In high school, everyone used to go back there after closing time to drink and make out and jump off the cliffs into the water twenty feet below. You went sometimes, but you never jumped, hating the way the girls would yell all the way down, hating the way their voices were extinguished in the water, and you, you alone, would be sure that they were dead on the rocks, or pinned against them by the current, down below the air. When they would scramble back up the trail, goose pimpled in their bikinis, streaked with dust, you knew that you were alone with the knot in your stomach, the chastened sense of a horror barely avoided. Eventually a boy did die there—some boy you had not known, a year after you graduated. When you read it in the paper, you had wanted to call someone, to tell them you had been right all along about the awful thing that was waiting in that place. Then, the next day, the paper said he did not hit the rocks at all; the water had been cold and the shock of it had stopped his heart. Or maybe the fall. By then, there hadn't been anyone to call anyway.

Your mother has come up behind you and stands with her arms crossed on her chest, one hand up with fingers spread open over her heart.

"Oh dear," she says.

"What?" you say, and she just points out towards the gray line of the rain. Now you see that the green of the land is spotted with dark ovals and hourglasses. You had noticed these marks and known them to be water, but you had not thought how strange this was—not swollen rivers or tidal pools, just water seeping up through the pores of the earth, making an uncanny wetland of the foothills and the mountain slopes. Now you think that maybe there is water beneath your feet—a falls or a spring or a new sea waiting to gush out into the valley—and you wonder, if you jumped, whether there would be a pool to swallow you.

"It's moving in already," she says. "Maybe we should go down."

"Okay," you say, but find yourself reluctant to move from your perch; the ground below your boots feels soft, untrustworthy. Your mother walks past you, out to the very edge, and then, impossibly, beyond. The bright spot of her blond head bobs then disappears. Her voice comes up to you, calling your name, and so you go forward and find that the ledge is really just a long slope, crisscrossed by trails. She is standing ten feet below you, having jogged down the hill at its steepest point instead of walking around to where the paths connected.

"This way will be faster," she says, "but it is a bit more treacherous."

"I'm used to treachery," you say, shimmying down the slope to join her.

You begin to walk side by side; the path is wide here. She flicks her face towards you, and then away again.

"Are you being glib, Jane?' she says.

"You brought me up here to talk about something, didn't you? Maybe you should start talking."

"You're not making it easy for me."

You snort at this, and you see her pinch her little lips together, flutter her eyes in a way that might mean tears. She breathes deeply, and you look away from her, embarrassed by her sheepishness and her fear. The dark clouds are edging in closer, but above you the sky is brilliant, an opalescent gray filled heavy with a light it will not release, a Chinese-lantern sky.

"I have always hoped that as you got older you would come to understand," she says, turning your head back towards her, in spite of you, "but I see now that you probably never will. I have processed all of this a long time ago, and I am done feeling guilty about my choices. You are alone in that now." She enunciates this slowly and carefully, a stage whisper, a sound meant to carry.

"That's not fair," you say, and she nods.

"No, it's not," she says, and you see the words, "But life isn't fair, honey," forming in her throat and in her eyes, and you are sure that is what she means to say when she opens her mouth, but somehow the words are changed as they mingle into the damp chill of the air. "But it wouldn't have been fair if I'd stayed either," she says, "if I had kept myself and Mara in that situation when I could have gone. I couldn't stay for you, not when I had my other daughter to think about. And myself. Is that so wrong?" She is staring at you and you can feel the blood rushing to your cheeks and your fingertips. You want to move towards her, to touch her, to back her away.

"You were the mother. It was your job to stay for me."

There is something you love in fighting, the way the words come out of you thoughtlessly, a function of your body.

"Maybe someday you'll learn that being a mother doesn't always mean you're cut out to be a martyr too," she says. "I did a wrong thing to you, I know. But I have been a good mother to your sister, and a good wife to Steve, and a good neighbor and friend, and if I hadn't done that one bad thing then I couldn't have been a good woman for the rest of my life. I've made up for it now."

"Not to me," you say.

She is getting flustered. Her hands shake. Her voice has gone thin and sweet. You are afraid of being convinced by her, her suffering.

"Do you think I could have stopped him if I'd stayed? Could I have stopped him from hurting you? He hit me, you know. He broke my arm once. Do you even know what was happening to me in that house? And what about Mara? How long would he have left her alone?"

"I was a child, and you left me with that man." You will not be kind to her. You will not allow yourself to see her through her own eyes, a woman wrong in degree rather than in kind.

"I didn't leave you. He kept you. He wouldn't let you go. He'd have come after us. He'd never have let us get away from him if I'd tried to take you too. He was distracted with you, and that's the only reason we got out. I wish that wasn't true, but it is. I don't think you know what he's capable of."

You think you will probably just laugh at this, at how ludicrous it is, how deluded. You think you will laugh, long, derisive, cruel—but when you try, you just can't find it funny. Not a bit.

"You're a fucking monster," you say, and she hardens. She is walking beside you. She has turned her eyes away. You edge your body away from hers on the trail, afraid of your hands brushing. Your words have transfigured her into something truly frightening. Her little body seems stretched tight, her bones straining against her skin. It is so long before she says anything that you forget there is a way out of this silence. The moment feels stretched wide, a valley hemmed in by rain. Now and again, a drop falls on your face or your arm. These drops are cold, and you feel them as they slide from your body, leaving trails.

"What makes you think," she says, "that your life is more important than our lives? Your sister's and mine?"

You pluck an answer out of the air, out of the babbling, incoherent cloud of answers that swarm you, their feet on your skin, and their teeth in your flesh.

"Because," you say, "that's what my father taught me."

The rain comes soon after that, a slushy drizzle that turns to sleet, the ice catching in your hair, stinging. It becomes quickly unbearable, and you both begin to run—a quarter mile to the car, perhaps a third. She is never more than a few yards ahead, and you know she is slowing herself for your sake. Still, when you reach the car you feel a pain in your chest unlike anything you've ever known—a cold that feels ripped open or ripping out, a hardness in your lungs that is too big to breathe into and seems to want to escape you. You double over against the hood and want to cry—do cry, you think, though it is lost amongst your awful gasping. Your mother leans over from the driver's side to unlock your door. You climb in and sit, fiddling at the heater, already turned as high as it will go, the vent pointed as straight at your heart as you can get it. Your clothes feel like the skin of some dead thing decaying on you; you would like to rip them off, but you glance at your mother beside you and leave them, hating the feeling.

You turn out of the parking lot and onto the main route. You are amazed how quickly the roads begin to flood. The rain is met as it falls by the water surging up from the sodden ground, and deluge is met by deluge until the surface of the earth becomes a swirling friction plane squeezed between the low disk of the sky and the hard rock that lies just inches below the grass, unforgiving of the inundation. Your mother sits hunched over the wheel, staring hard through the window that appears with each pass of the windshield wipers, the scene revealing itself in fits and starts, a stop-motion tableau of a worsening disaster. Flows of mud are replaced by downed tree branches and plastic trashcans washed into the street. Beside you, a stream has overflowed its banks and rips clods of earth into its current. In the scars the water leaves, you glimpse a few last bits of color in a growing whiteness. Finally, there is only deep water through which the road is hardly distinguishable and the low purr of the tires tossing up waves.

Your mother is trying to be quiet, but her teeth have begun to chatter; through them, she is releasing a low, unintentional hum, the sound of her body's shivering forcing the air from her lungs. It is a terrible sound, a sick sound, and you want to tell her to pull over and let you drive, but some part of you still feels so frozen and scared that you can't choose to do anything at all.

When, finally, she pulls the car into the driveway, Steve comes running out to meet you, the hood of his rain jacket pulled tight around his face.

"Did you girls get caught in this? You're like a couple of drowned rats," he says, and his voice is so loud after your quiet, so broad and happy, that it catches you like a blow, like a tightening in your stomach. You wish you could hug him with your hands spread a ruler's length apart over his broad back, just for overlooking you so easily.

"I was worried about you out there on the road," he says. "Lights are out, sorry to say, but at least it wasn't you guys wrapped around the pole, you know?" He stands up straight and taps the top of the car with the flat of his hand. "I don't think it's stopping, ladies. Time to make a run for it."

You pull yourself up out of the car and set off for the house at a jog. Water pours into your shoes; it runs in a wide, ankle-deep stream through the yard. A pumpkin is pinned against the fence, twirling in an eddy.

Inside, Steve has set up an ancient radio near his armchair in the living room. He sits there listening, adjusting the antenna when the signal grows weak, and occasionally feeding wood into the fireplace. Your mother has changed into flannel pajamas and is fluttering around the house, searching for candles and inventorying her emergency preparedness kits. Now and again, Steve calls her into the living room to listen to the radio with him. "This is a big one," he says again and again.

You hear this all from the bed in Mara's room where you are rolled tight into a comforter, a towel spread across your pillow to catch the water from your hair, which is thick and heavy like a horse tail and takes hours to dry. You are warm now, except for the tips of your ears and your nose, and your limbs feel liquid and useless. You do not feel like a creature who has ever moved. You strain to listen to the radioman's voice, but it is only a murmur in which you can often hear the words but rarely make out the meaning. There are strings of numbers, highways or school districts or inches, and the words "closures" and "evacuations."

The sun sets, or is dissolved completely into the storm, and then the room is very dark, darker than it has ever been, perhaps, the moonless sky reflecting no artificial illumination, no human afterglow. You are exhausted, and the darkness carries you down into a drowning sleep from which you awaken confused, the sounds of voices and rain muddled in your head—a container from which the contents have suddenly vanished. Your mother is in the doorway, already speaking.

"I'll just put it here by the door," she says. You do not know what time it is. You are on an island in time.

"Okay," you say, sitting halfway up and discovering a sore spot in your back. "That's fine." You think you may have known, a few moments before, what she was talking about, but it is gone from you now.

"I'm sorry to have to tell you all this. The news is vague, so nothing is for sure. It looks like you should be able to get back to the highway tomorrow, but you might be stuck if you stay any longer than that. Everything west of here is closed already. We'll know by afternoon whether we can stay."

"I'll go in the morning," you say.

She is lingering. You can barely see her, but you hear her nails drumming softly on the wood of the doorframe.

"Jane," she says, "I don't like this."

"I don't either," you say.

The drumming stops, and you think she is gone though you do not hear her go.

"Do you need anything?" she says.

You say, "I need money."

Though she does not say anything to this, you can hear the skin-rustle of her hand pulling away from the door, can feel the vibration of her feet in the hall, and can imagine, in the final, drifting moment of consciousness, the sound of a pen shaping zeroes on a check.

6

It rains for ten hours straight, and you do not stop driving, save for once, when the needle of your gas gauge has hovered over the E for so long that you begin to wonder if it is broken. Perhaps the deluge has caused it to short circuit, you think. Maybe it has never meant anything at all. Then a gas station emerges in front of you, glowing orange and god-sent, and the attendants come streaming out to your car, three of them at once with jackets and newspapers held over their heads as they run from the door of their building to the cover of the little roof overtop the pumps, from which the water cascades so heavily that standing by your car is like standing behind a waterfall. They are soaked to the knees and big eyed; there has been some excitement. They are three young men—three boys— and they stare in at you with a guileless amazement, as if your appearance in that place is something wholly miraculous, a visitation. One boy has raised his palm and seems ready to pound it flat against your window; you roll it down and say, "Fill it with regular."

The oldest one, the one who takes the pump from its handle and begins to fill your tank without a word, looks to be about seventeen. The other two are younger, rangy, and forward with you in a way you do not like. These two stand leaning against your door, pressing you with questions: where are you coming from and where are you going? What are the roads like? Have you heard any reports?

You know little and they are disappointed with you. You listened to the radio for an hour as you wound your way out of Mt Shasta on some side street, but you did not known the names of the roads they reported closed or threatened. You had calculated your chances of getting out of town purely on the quantity of the blocked passages, which seemed, in the last minutes before the air went dead, to be all of them. The first ten miles had been the hairiest, and when, finally, you had made it to the highway, you thought that you must have been getting ahead of it. But then for hours there had been no change at all—only a heavy stream that hardly bothered to divide into drops before being swept away by your wiper blades. It was hard to see, but there was no one else on the road, and you had gotten comfortable in the way you drifted in and out of lanes around the curves, hugging the yellow line, and then the white.

"Which way is it moving?" one of the boys asks, his freckled hands holding onto the window frame, fingers creeping in.

"Which way is that?" you ask, pointing back the way you've come.

"West," he says.

"It's worse to the west," you say. "It's bad in Mt. Shasta."

The boy stands up, looks at his companions. "We're fucking surrounded by it," he says, not to you.

"Did you get ahold of Joe?" the other boy says. "I think he needs to get out here."

"I couldn't get shit. I don't know whether it was on his end or mine."

You watch in the rearview mirror as the third boy finishes pumping your gas and returns the nozzle to its hook. He has dark scraggles of hair that have gotten wet and fallen into his eyes, and he shakes his head to dislodge them. He shakes again. He appears at your window and tells you the price, but when you reach into your wallet and pull out your debit card, he hesitates.

"The machines are all down," he says. "We didn't make a sign. Do you have cash?" Before you can answer, he shakes his head again. "Why don't you just take it," he says. "It doesn't...it's fine."

"Thank you," you say. "Is it bad that way?" You point to the road ahead.

"We've been here so long," the boy says. "I wish I could tell you."

You thank him again and turn your key in the ignition, relieved to hear the engine starting clean. You watch them in the mirror as you pull back onto the road, but they do not turn their faces from you. They stare after you as you go.

You go only half a mile before turning off into an empty strip-mall parking lot. The boys have unnerved you, and you want to hear Johnny's voice, to tether yourself to something beyond this drifting and this wash. You dial twice and hear nothing—no ring and no voice, only the hollow silence of the signal moving through space. "Hello," you say, "hello?" but not even an echo returns to you. You check your reception and try again, and now you hear a rasping mechanical tone, high and broken, resolving into a short ring. You welcome this noise.

"Jane?" you hear him say. "God. I was...Did you? Hello?"

"Hello," you say, "Johnny?"

"Jane...I....are you?"

His voice is dropping out every few words, falling back into the sea of static it reaches you through. When it emerges again, the voice sounds altered, some fragmented interference still clinging to it.

"Jane," he says.

"Johnny," you say. "I miss you. Can you hear me?"

"Insane," he says, "the news...nothing."

"I'm okay," you say. "Can you hear me?"

"Quiet," he says, and then the resolute beep of the call ending.

You sit for a moment, staring at the phone in your hand, the bars wavering between something and nothing. Above you, the sky is darker. If you have gotten ahead, you have not gotten far.

The phone rings. The tone is clear, and you answer.

"How is this?" you say. "Is this better?"

"Jane." The voice is ragged and deep. The static rises up around it.

"Johnny?" you say. This is not his voice.

"Jane. Jane."

"Who is this?" you say.

"...I've reached you... Don't worry...Jane."

You feel a quivering in your jaw, a shaking in your hands. There are noises on the line, thumping that may be in the connection and may be beyond it. The voice speaks again, garbled, unintelligible. You hear "Wait," you hear "Water," and you hear "Home."

You pull the phone from your ear while the voice is still speaking and push your fingers hard against the buttons until it is silent. The number is untraceable. Your signal is gone. The phone does not ring again.

You drive all day and into the evening. Around you, the land becomes a desert, and the rain persists. You see few people outside of the cities, and even there the highways are hung with an ominous quiet out of which each passing car emerges as a cacophony, a blur of movement against the uncanny stillness and the contemplative steadiness of the rain. The darkening sky drives you forward, out into the desolation beyond the edges of the towns. In the empty stretches of desert off the highway, you see cattle, hundreds of them gathered by the roadside, unrestrained by fences or wires. They stand in dense clusters, wide-eyed, lowing. A calf wanders in front of your car and you brake hard to miss it; it becomes afraid and will not move, but stands with its legs wide and planted, braying back at you as you lay on the horn. Finally, you go around. You wonder why they do not make for shelter or for higher ground. You joke to yourself that they could be wondering the same of you, but this does not lighten the memory of their big, dark bodies crowding together in the dim of the sunset, or the sound of their betrayed voices calling.

You stop when the rain does. It is hard to know the exact moment; it has grown lighter as you've wound your way down into one of the canyons, sheltered by the high, red-rock walls. When you emerge it is like waking; the clouds have cleared and there is a bright moon, but you notice the dry-glass squeal of your windshield wipers before you see the empty air and the dry ground around you. Your exhaustion pours over you, your body feeling like a muscle stretched too far, twanging in painful release. You promise yourself you'll stop at the next town, wherever that may be, but you barely make it five miles before you bob out of an open-eyed dream to find yourself drifting across the center line, hands fallen from the wheel.

You pull off to the side of the road and sleep for an hour, or sit hovering, just conscious, listening to the unpunctuated silence of the desert night. In your drifting, the desolation and the quiet wrap themselves into a deep and centerless music that you hear the way you hear thoughts, the way you sound out words in your head. From where you are, you do not wish to go farther. It is terribly beautiful in this sound, and you feel your mind pulling to a rest. As you listen, the sound opens itself into a landscape that is at once the empty Nevada road and a vision beyond it, an unpeopled world from which even you are absent. In all this is a wonderful rest, a deep sleep within your waking mind. You only know that you have slept at all by the way you jump when your music is broken by some real noise, lost as soon as you've heard it—a coyote yapping from somewhere nearby, the wind, or just your own ungainly shifting away from the cold and the slow ache forming in your hips. You sit for a while, hoping to regain the sanctity of the lost moment, but you have been unmistakably returned to a world shrunk back into its boundaries.

You find a hotel a half-hour later, in one of those desert towns that exist for no purpose except to assist you in leaving, placed for no reason but distance from any place like it—from any place at all. There is a gas station and an all-night diner franchise. There is a grocery store, and a hotel, and, in the hotel, a bar. A person could spend their whole life here; your life has not been so different from this. Inside you are surprised to find a lobby full of light and noise, a dozen people lounging around a fuzzed-out TV. They are dressed in pajamas and holding drinks, and they all smile at you as you enter. You smile back, but find yourself hesitating at the door, afraid that you have stumbled into a place you do not belong, dreading the explanations and, even more, the cold of the road. You have been thinking of a hot bath and a room with king-size bed. You would like to spend some of your mother's money on these things; you would like to buy a big dinner in the barroom and share it with these strangers.

You feel overwhelmed by the light and the sound, and you miss The Pauline's welcome, the cold simplicity of the place that had been held onto beyond reason and comfort. You have forgotten what she looked like now, in her portrait, and instead she is like a sapling tree in your memory, like something bent over in the wind. You imagine her emerging from some little back room, some lonely prairie house, some crack in the world, the lines in her face deep deep deep, and she is ready to take you in to her empty, consuming world.

A woman appears behind the check-in counter and gestures you forward. She is not much older than you are, but there is something in the grave expression of her face and the heavy movements of her body that make you sigh with the relief of her presence, her obvious authority.

"Do you have any vacancies?" you say, not sure if you have even said hello. You find that you want a room badly. The need has grown in you; it has become vital.

"No," she says, shaping the severe curve of her lips into a smile, "not as such. But we won't turn anyone away tonight."

"Oh," you say, startled, glancing back at the group behind you, noticing the bed-sheets and blankets spread out on the floor between them.

"It's a lot of families, but I think there were a couple other single girls who might split with you. If not, we're out of cots, but there are plenty of duvets left. A couple of them on the carpet really isn't too bad. That's what I'll be doing."

"All right," you say, feeling a shock of embarrassment, as if you have intruded upon a suffering. "Anything, I guess."

"It might take a little while to figure out who's in what room. People have been swapping, and we're trying to make sure the older folks get proper beds, but I'll let you know if I find you something. Till then, the bedding is there by the vending machines, and the bathroom and the bar are at the end of this hall." She gestured with a nod of her chin. "You can set up anywhere you like. I know it's noisy here, but you might want to be nearby in case there is any news."

"Okay," you say. You have had your hand in your purse all this while, fingering the bills in your wallet, but you see now how strange it would seem to offer her money for what, it appears, is not a luxury but a basic kindness, a harbor. You want to ask what has happened to these people, but she looks up into your eyes, lips pursed thin.

"Where are you coming from, honey?" she says.

"Oregon," you say. "Lincoln City. I left two days ago."

"That's lucky," she says, and you see her eyes looking into yours, a tightening in her jaw. You are on the edge of asking, but do not.

"Yes," you say. "It's not even raining here."

She nods, very serious, the hard lines of her face stretching out into long furrows.

"God willing," she says.

Of course, you wouldn't be let go so easily. There has always been something to keep you, to drag you home. Your father had told you as much, during your first, fluttering attempts to get away.

"I think I'm going to take a week off from work next month," you said over dinner one night, as you sat side by side with him, your sleeves brushing as you reached for the salt, the butter, another serving of beans.

"And why's that?" he said. He didn't look up from his plate. There was nothing in his voice to alarm you—no anger, no jealousy—and yet you heard something enter, an edge of coldness, a calculation.

"I want to go visit Mara," you said. "She's in school. In Pennsylvania. Well, she's on break right now, I guess." Mara had wanted you to make up a story to tell him. She didn't want him finding out where she lived. But you didn't want to lie and didn't want to be caught lying, and so you told him the truth, trying to keep your voice as plain and still as you could. He'd never shown any interest in her anyway. If he'd wanted her back, he'd have gotten her.

He doesn't say anything at all, and you talk nervously to fill the space, your worst habit.

"The tickets aren't all that bad, and I'd be staying at her house, so I wouldn't have too many other expenses. I have enough saved up, anyhow, and I can pick up a few shifts. It's not like I've ever had a real vacation before," you said. "I'll report back and tell you if it's worth trying."

He looked up at you then, his lips pressed tight beneath his beard. He stared into you for a long while, and neither of you spoke. He got up and took his plate to the sink. You heard the water turn on and the whisper of a steel brush against ceramic. You stayed at the table, your hands resting on either side of your half-empty plate, your fingernails gripping.

"Do you think that sounds okay?" you said, speaking loud to cover the crack in your voice. For a while, he still said nothing, but then the water turned off and he came out and leaned in the doorway, wiping his hands on a dishtowel.

"Sure," he said, his voice slow and hard. "I think it's okay. I think someday you were bound to figure out there was a world out there that you wanted to see. And I think you're going to realize real quick that it's not for you. This place is so deep in you, Janie. You won't last a day anywhere else. You'll wash away as soon as there's no salt to hold you together."

"I'm not moving there," you said, refusing to look at him, your eyes on the table. "It's just a vacation."

"That's right, babe," he said, chuckling as he turned back into the kitchen. "That's god-damn, mother-fucking right."

You didn't talk about your trip again, but he started sending you links to newspaper articles, and you'd read them in the hour after you got home from work, as he puttered around in his shed before dinner. They were a litany of disasters: fires, floods, massacres—stories about what happened to people out in that big world. There was one about a Pennsylvania college girl who had been kidnapped, beaten, raped, killed, and left by the side of the road in a little country town. Above this story, he had written, "be careful."

You sit on the floor at the edge of the group, unsure of whether you want this or any other company. You wrap yourself in the blanket you've been given, though you are not really cold in this room, so dense with bodies and breath. The blanket is heavy, cheap, and plastic to the touch; it makes you feel like the refugee you are slowly discovering you are. You feel heavy and rooted down into the carpet, either afraid to move or finally contented in your stillness. You do not know which. You try to call Johnny again, as soon as you find a quiet place in the hall to sit, pressing your opposite ear closed with your palm and listening for the tinny, distant ring. A round-faced man walking past you on his way to the bathroom laughs when he sees your phone and says, "Good luck with that" in so cold a voice that you wonder if already this place has developed rules, etiquettes, a whole list of unspokens to render you ignorant and ill-fitting. You put the phone away; it isn't working anyhow. You make no more excursions after that; you stay close to your fellow displaced.

Around you, stories are swapped: homes abandoned, relatives unreachable, frightening rumors from the west—but some say east. You all sit in a circle and try to sort out what you know the way you would sort the pieces of a jigsaw puzzle, working from the edges in. A dark-haired man is telling of how he awoke to the radio telling him his town, fifty miles to the north of the hotel, was being evacuated. He'd gone to the window and looked out on a blue-skied day, the kids playing in the soft, warm air.

"We went anyway," he says. "I know how quick things can go south."

He hadn't heard anything since about the situation at home and was beginning to doubt there was really much of a disaster at all. "We haven't seen a drop of rain all week," he says. "I'd like to know if this has all been necessary."

It seems most people in the group are from somewhere nearby, making a preemptive move to the hotel's higher ground, spooked by the few dire and confused news reports that have reached them.

"I don't know if it's coming here, but they got caught off guard in the Pacific Northwest, and I'm not taking chances," a young woman says, staring at her hands in her lap, lifting the fingers one by one, as if exercising them.

"What did you hear about that?" you say, trying to keep the sharpness out of your voice. You have been reluctant to add anything to the conversation, to share your experiences or your fears, begrudging the inevitable interrogation.

"I heard it's gone," she says.

A heavy-set woman is speaking from an armchair in a tone of gleeful self-satisfaction, saying the whole thing swept through Mexico a week ago, leaving a swath of sunken cities, each one a new Atlantis—warnings as loud as air-raid sirens. She's been expecting this for years, she says.

"The real wonder," she adds, nodding her head in time to her words, "is that it didn't happen until now. We had plenty of time to prepare," she says. "It's our own damn fault that we didn't."

"You sound so happy about it," you say. She looks at you with her eyebrows pulled up to the part in her hair, smiling sad and sweet.

"Sometimes, baby girl," she says, "you've just got to take a longer view."

Waiting in the airport in Philadelphia, you were afraid that you would not recognize your sister. She'd described, over the phone the night before, her new haircut and the red hoodie she would be wearing. You'd written it down in your pocket notebook and said, "What letters are on the back again?"

"It doesn't matter," she'd said. "I'm going to know who you are."

"It's been a long time, Mara," you'd said. "I've changed a bit."

"You haven't," she'd said. "I can tell."

Sitting on a cold plastic chair with your bag between your feet, you wanted badly not to show how right you thought she was—how much you felt the world had moved beyond your ability to live in it as you stayed immobilized, quickly antiquating. You had decided not to tell Mara that this was the farthest you had ever been from home, that this was your first plane ride, your first time east of the Rockies, the Mississippi, the West. She'd guess it all, probably, but she was your little sister. You wouldn't say.

You were terrified on the airplane. On the train up to Portland, you'd told yourself that flying would be no different, just more empty hours in a metal tube, but it wasn't the same at all. You could feel the gravity in your skin. You could not forget where you were. You sat wedged between two gray-haired men in nice suits who seemed bored into a kind of comfortable non-existence, as dependable and soothing as the smiling figures in the safety pamphlet. They worked on laptops, sipped vodka tonics, and stood up to stretch their legs in the aisles every hour. You did not speak to each other except for the excuse-mes and thank-yous as one or another of you squeezed past the rest. Still, you would see it when their eyes met over you, when you flinched at the dipping of the wings or the quiet following what you took to be the stalling of the engine. In those moments, you would see how ridiculous you appeared to them, too old to be so frightened. You ordered a glass of wine from the flight attendant, but it was barely noon, and drinking it made you feel sick and woozy.

You'd left your house an hour before dawn that morning and had barely slept the night before. Your dad was supposed to drive you to the airport, but as the day had gotten closer, he had grown moodier, quicker to anger, and to apologize tenderly and abjectly afterwards. A scene was coming, and you'd guessed that the drive was the time he had appointed to make it. Though it would make things worse when you got back, you'd set your alarm for two hours early and hid it under your pillow so he wouldn't hear. You'd grabbed your bags and bolted out of the house in your pajamas, changing your clothes and brushing your teeth in the train station bathroom.

Though you'd felt shaky and stretched-out all day, you weren't able to sleep on the plane. In Philadelphia, you felt like the whole world was slipping away from you, flattening like a piece of paper being smoothed between fingers. You had never felt so tired. Still, there was something pleasurable in this—a loosening of tension, a feeling of relief all out of proportion to the accomplishment of getting on and off a cross-country flight. You had told your father that you would call him from the airport, as soon as your plane touched down, but you did not do this.

The television flickers from white to black, and for a moment a figure appears—a man in a suit with a microphone. He's appeared off and on throughout the night, sometimes speaking and sometimes silent, sometimes whole and sometimes ripped into pieces by the static and spread into his component parts across the screen—the pinkish blur of his collar intersecting the suburban street behind him while his eyes make for the upper left corner. The people in the room shush each other when he appears, though you have watched for an hour and learned nothing. He was clearest in a three-minute stretch shortly after you arrived: standing in front of a modest ranch house, he told about a boy who had slipped into a swollen storm drain and been carried a half mile. The reception had paled, and you had not heard the end of the story.

Now he is standing in front of a darkened office building, moving his arm in long, slow circles, open-palmed, indicating something—a range. His voice falters between the comprehensible and the metallic. He puts his hand to his ear, pausing to listen to some unknown message. The sound improves.

"Power has been out here for the last six hours. It is estimated that at least forty-thousand homes and businesses have been affected in the area, though Northwest Electric has been unable to provide an accurate number. The Governor has declared a state of emergency."

"Where is this?" someone behind you asks. "Where is this broadcasting from?"

"In addition to the outages, we can assume there has been some serious damage to the power infrastructure that could potentially take weeks to repair. Authorities are now recommending that even residents not directly affected by the flooding evacuate if they do not have access to working communication devices."

"Evacuate to where?" the woman beside you says. "How are they supposed to even get the message to evacuate?"

"This is unprecedented," the newsman says. He pauses and turns his head, pressing his palm against his ear. "The situation is expected to worsen overnight," he says. "I'm just being told this now."

"Where are you?" someone howls out from the hush of the room. "Tell us where you are." But the man is already gone, dissolved into a disembodied murmur and then into the gentle hissing that you all let play out around you, the volume turned up as high as it will go.

"Jane!" she yelled when she spotted you, her voice shriller and younger than it had sounded on the phone. You stood up and saw her then, pushing her way towards you. You thought that just maybe you would have recognized her after all. Maybe there was something inside you that knew her among everyone—the reuniting lovers, and the young women yelling into phones, and the drivers with their cardboard signs, and the angry men pushing the luggage carts, yelling at everyone to move out of the way, and your sister, Mara, waving.

On the drive back to her house, you kept catching yourself staring out the window, trying to catalogue the known and unknown elements of the landscape.

"See anything interesting?" Mara asked, and it was then you realize she had been talking, had been trying to tell you something.

"I'm sorry," you said. "I'm a little disoriented."

"A lot different?" she said, flicking her face towards you, looking proud.

"It looks just like home," you said.

"Does it?"

She smiled and faced ahead, squinting a little at a shadow on the road, and you wished you had not said anything. She had good reason to be proud; your family had never been one that wandered far. You remembered a day in high school when your teacher had explained that until the invention of cars and passenger trains, most people never traveled more than twenty miles from the place they were born. Everyone in the class had laughed like it was the most ridiculous thing they'd ever heard, but you'd sat and tried to think of the names of the towns twenty miles away from your own and found that you could not. Still, it did look just like home, even if Mara would not see that or could not remember: low hills folded into the feet of mountains and stretched out into fields. From a distance, the tree lines blurred together and looked like forests. You were disappointed; you wanted to be changed. You wanted the land to become strange to you.

Mara seemed happy, anyway. After twenty minutes, she told you she had decided she wouldn't be going back to school the next fall. She hated the falling-down industrial city the college sat in the middle of, the manicured campus lawns a mean joke on the decay and the waste all around them. She hated the stuck-up kids for whom going to this expensive private college meant nothing at all. She hated not knowing what she wanted to study, and she hated the hoops she had to jump through to convince the college she was still worthy of their scholarship money. She hated the way they made her feel that she had failed.

"I met better people," she said. "People I can actually stand to live with." She smiled at you, as if you knew all about this, her troubles with living. "You're going to love our house," she said, drawing big pictures in the air with her hands. Do you do this? Does your mother? "It's out in the middle of nowhere. Actual nowhere. We have a huge garden and a giant yard with a creek, and the whole thing is renting for less than a two-bedroom near the college. There aren't, like, tons of hippie posers around, either. All our neighbors are old dutchy people—old farmers who smoke four packs a day."

"Dutchy?" you said.

"Pennsylvania Dutch. That's what people are out here. It means German."

"Like the Amish?"

"No," she said, "it's different."

You disappeared farther out into the country—the sticks, your dad would say—and the highways gave way to Routes and these to Ways and Lanes. The road, too, deteriorated, from macadam into gravel and finally into a pebbly dust that was once blacktop. All around were fields, knee-high wheat and rich, plowed earth, and here and there the nubbin of something growing, the color of lime candy. Mara pulled off the road beside a mailbox and pulled out a stack of letters. She held them up in front of her face, scanned the names as she picked her way up the long sloping drive, and then flicked them one by one into the back seat. You had the feeling she was putting on some sort of show for you.

"I don't think these people live here anymore," she said.

"You're not sure?"

"Well," she said, grinning, the sun streaming in from over the trees and lighting her face like a paper lantern, "it's a fluid household. People go by different names sometimes."

At the top of the drive was an old stone farmhouse. Set back in the trees, it looked as if it had been in that spot longer than the forest—so settled it had begun to sag. Dirty lace curtains hung in all the windows, and cars squeezed in around the door at odd angles, some with their hoods propped open, others on blocks, most just looking tired and dented.

"Full house today," Mara said. "It looks like we have some travelers." She nodded to a truck next to you as you opened your door—a huge and ageless Ford. In the bed of the truck, someone appeared to have built a small cottage out of plywood, sheet metal, and rollout insulation. The "house" stood about eight feet over the back of the truck, attached with a complex of screws and weld marks and bungee cables. It looked *precarious. There were two Plexiglas windows cut into the side of the structure, and, at the back, a door on which someone had painted a number—101—and below that, in elegant cursive script, "The Manor."*

"I'll ask Johnny to show you the inside," Mara said. "It's pretty amazing. He's got a whole apartment in there. There's a mini fridge, even."

"Your roommate?" you said.

"No," she said. "Sometimes."

"Does he pay rent?" you said.

She laughed and shook her head, red hair falling into her eyes. You could not tell if it was the effect of the sunlight or if she'd dyed it. You did not remember it being so much lighter than your own.

"Then he's not a roommate," you said, wondering how long you could maintain this, this stance of knowing things about the world. You said it with a laugh so that she would not know exactly what you meant, would not know whether you were dispensing sisterly advice or representing some small view of the world that she'd already outgrown.

"That's not really how it works around here," she said. "You'll see. We try to keep things looser than that. I mean, what, did Dad pay rent?" This last part was said softly. It was an inching forward.

"Sometimes," you said. "But Dad isn't really a roommate either."

She smiled, and the backs of your hands banged together as you both reached the porch stairs.

"Sorry," she said.

She pushed open the unlocked door and led you into a small foyer lined with racks of shoes—muddy hiking boots and worn-out sneakers with holes in the toes or the soles. The shelves that circled the room above your head were stuffed with an impossible clutter of boxes, spilling the sleeves of sweaters or the wrinkled pages of notebooks. Mara slipped off her shoes and kicked them into a corner, and, after a moment, you did the same, surprised by the chill of the stone floor through your socks. A glass-paned door led you into a sunny kitchen, large but crowded-over with herbs blooming in cracked pots and things dried and sealed in mason jars.

"Hello?" Mara called out, but the words fell heavy and dead in the air. No one answered. "They must have all gone somewhere together," she said, lips pursed, and then was quiet for a moment. "Well, you'll meet them later," she said, turning to smile at you. "Do you want some tea? We have about a bazillion varieties."

"I'm okay," you said, sitting down at a wide, green table and staring out the window, which looked across a blooming, overgrown back yard. "This place is huge, Mara. How do you afford all this?" you said.

She shrugged, struggling to hide her pride at your interest.

"No one wants to live out in the middle of nowhere," she said, leaning against the stove as she talked, her arms braced behind her back, "so it's not that bad. Plus, we don't have to pay for that much besides rent. We try to do a lot of bartering. It's

amazing how much easier everything is when you pool your resources. It just feels crazy sometimes, to think of the way so many people live by themselves or in pairs, with a few kids maybe. We're pack animals. We're meant to help each other."

"How many people live here?" you said. You would not say to her the reasons you knew to live alone, the reasons to be distrustful of packs.

"Well, there are five of us here full time and paying rent, and then there's Amy, who's mostly full time, but she doesn't work or have school so she contributes by being our housewife and doing a lot of cleaning and cooking and stuff. She used to be Johnny's partner, which is how he started coming around, but I think she kind of wigged out on the traveling stuff. Which is weird because what were you expecting from the house-truck guy?"

"I guess I wouldn't really know what to expect from a house-truck guy," you said, marveling at her—at how deeply she had settled into the knowledge of this new life, at how trusting she was.

"Well, he's still a traveler, even if he isn't as grimy as the train hoppers," she said.

"People still do that?" you said. "Like hobos?"

"I know, right? I really want to try, but I'm scared I'd get a leg cut off or something."

She took a kettle from the stove and filled it with water, and you did not stop her. She set it back on the burner, and you did not mention that she had forgotten to turn on the flame. You had not considered, until this moment, that she might feel nervous around you—that she might be struggling to reach all these words around your silent presence.

"But whatever, Johnny's cool," she said, "and he's the best dumpster diver ever. Every time he comes here, he brings us bags and bags of groceries. Good stuff too—organic veggies and fancy cheese and stuff. I guess he goes to a lot of co-ops and hippie places like that because they're cool with people re-using and don't throw bleach on their dumpsters like the big chain places do. There are a lot of bands who come through too. We have some neo-vaudeville punk guys here right now who my roommate Jesse knows. They're pretty cool. You'll like them."

"Where does everyone sleep?" you said.

"Wherever," she shrugged. "We find places. You can share my bed. I'm the lonely girl right now."

"You don't seem it," you said.

She shrugged again, stretching her lips into a thin smile.

You fall asleep behind a sofa in the lobby, lulled by the sounds of a dozen bodies breathing. You waited hours, but it had become clear that no beds would open. Every few minutes a new face would arrive in the huddle around the TV, coming from rooms or quiet hallways to check if anything new had been learned. Nothing had. The newsman did not emerge again, at least not while you were awake, though you do retain a phantasmal impression of him—of his deep and soothing voice—culled either from half-awake remembrances or from dreams. No one came in from outside. You were the last. You are afraid now, certain you should never have left home. You should have known—did know—that something awful would happen. You think you are forgetting Johnny bit by bit and falling back into something that will keep you. You see closed-eyed visions of yourself and Pauline, alone together in an empty place, happy enough, you suppose. You think you have pushed already too far outside the life you were meant for. "Tomorrow," you tell yourself, "I will turn around." You do not think this is a promise you mean to keep, but it calms you. Sometime after the lights are turned off and you lay drifting, you hear one of your neighbors speaking in a stage whisper.

"Do you think they heard something, out there?"

The last thoughts you recall before sleep are the twinned questions: Who? Where?

The roommates and whoever-elses came in a few hours later, as you were cleaning up the dinner Mara had made you—rice and vegetables in some sort of improvised sauce, mixed by intuition from unlabeled mason jars of pungent, earth-colored liquids and tiny, nameless seeds. They came in making a lot of noise, laughing, and jumping in on each other's jokes. It made the house reverberate; the two of you had been very quiet.

"Whiskey and donuts," one of them said, a small guy with dark hair that fell into his face and across his greasy, pointed chin.

"It's a weekly thing now," said another, a blond girl in cutoff jeans and moccasins. She had a wide, warm face, and you found yourself smiling into it

"Last week we figured out when the Dunkin Donuts throws away the leftovers," Mara said. "Then we bought some whiskey."

"You're Jane," said a girl with short-cropped hair. "I'm Allie." Or maybe it was Jamie, or even Annie. They all introduced themselves then, but ten minutes later, you wouldn't remember the names. It will be disconcerting to realize, later, that Johnny was there among them, that he looked into your face and touched your hand, and you did not recognize him. On that first moment of your introduction, he left no trace of what he would be to you.

They made a fire in the back yard, and you sat with them for hours, drinking whiskey from the bottle and smoking heavy, dark weed that smelled like mushrooms and tasted like dirt. Later, there was a jug of wine that stained your chapped lips the color of dried blood. A plastic bag of stale donuts was offered every now and again, but you couldn't bring yourself to take one. Your stomach felt full of air and bubbles. For a while, Mara was sitting across the fire pit from you; whenever your eyes met she would look at you so hard, as if she was trying to make everyone else disappear so she could tell you a secret. You could only stand that for so long before you would start to giggle, and, once you did, her face would crack open and she would laugh like a crazy woman until you couldn't even look at each other without doubling over. Everyone else started to ask what it was about and to think, paranoid, that it was about them.

At some point, hours in, Mara said she was going to pee and made for the woods, walking straight but with a kind of prideful concentration that gave her away. She was gone for a long time, and you sat quietly, watching everyone talk. You tried to hold the words in your head long enough to respond, but found that you could not. Then even the voices turned indecipherable; you knew the words but their meanings dissolved instantly, like ice in boiling water, and you were left with only the sounds to piece, bit by bit, back into a language you knew. Everything felt impossibly removed—a diorama world, stuck motionless behind glass. You began to feel afraid then and told them you were going to the bathroom too. Instead, you went back inside and lay down on the sofa, trying to feel the different parts of your body, the muscles tensing and the blood flowing underneath, and to know these as your own.

At some point, you looked up and saw him sitting beside you, though you had not heard him come in. He sat with his legs crossed on the upholstery—Indian style, you'd always heard it called, though you were probably among the last generation of American schoolchildren to know it by that name. He was staring ahead to the wall, and you thought for a moment that he was asleep despite the straightness of his back. You had seen him by the fire, but this is the moment that you would identify, in your sober reflections, as First Sight.

"You doing okay?" he said, turning towards you. His voice was higher and smoother than you'd expected from his bulk, his bearded face. It is hard to know exactly what you saw of him then; you certainly noticed his eyes, brown and rich and set so deep in his face that his round cheeks almost eclipsed them when he laughed. You probably saw, too, the thickness of his arms beneath the thin fabric of his white shirt, the dirty fingernails, and the hands that had done work. Maybe you had even sensed something of the monk in him—the deep quietude, the acceptance with which he approached all the creatures of the earth. You are sure, however, that if you had noticed none of these things, you would have wanted him just the same. You had never been before, and never expected to be again, thunderstruck.

"I'm okay," you said, sitting up quickly, feeling suddenly exposed to him. He was still looking into your face, and though you did not feel he needed you to go on, you did, afraid to leave the silence whole. "I don't usually smoke very much," you said. "That's all."

"Me neither," he said. "I understand." Though you immediately identified this as a lie, you felt your heart beat faster at the very suggestion of having someone like you in this strange place.

"Thanks for letting me stay here," you said. "Mara seems really happy with all of you."

"She's a happy girl," he said, lifting his shoulders in an exaggerated shrug, "but I don't live here. I'm just a frequent visitor."

"Are you the house-truck guy?" you said, though in fact you did, now, remember his name.

"Please," he said, "that's my father's name. Call me Johnny." He grinned as he said this, and you had laughed well before you understood the joke.

"Mara said it was a pretty cool truck," you said. He soothed you. You were sinking back into yourself, your body.

"So I'm told," he said—that elongated shrug again, the same grin. It seemed strangely affected, and this intrigued you. You wanted to strip away the layers of his contentment. "I am biased in its favor. Did you want to go have a look?"

"Sure," you said, "I'd love to." Already you were determined.

The inside of the truck was dense and warm—a miniature world, at once practical and enchanting. Pots and pans were arranged in milk crates under the bed, held fast with bungee cords. A counter and fridge were attached to the wall by some invisible machinations, and on top of them were stacked boxes of books and extension cords and a set of tools—the ephemera of a lived-in place. You felt for a moment that being in this space was like being inside his body—a womb or a vantage point—but then you realized it was only like being in a home.

"I got the idea for it from a guy I met in Vermont," he said, when the two of you were knee-to-knee in the small space of his bunk, surrounded by the tight press of the things he owned. "It was a bit of an investment, but I never have to pay for a hotel or worry about camping out in the rain again. If you travel as much as I do, it's worth it."

"How much do you travel?" you said, feeling a sharp stab of abandonment, reasonless as it was.

"It varies. A lot right now. I got here last weekend, and I'm leaving tomorrow to go visit some friends in Connecticut. Usually I go home in the winter and hunker down there for a while to earn some money. It gets cold in here, and I'm not a hundred-percent sure it's safe to use the stove. Installation was a little touch-and-go."

He nodded his head towards the corner behind you, and you turned to see an old-fashioned wood stove tucked in between a sink and a miniature restaurant booth.

"Where's home?" you said.

"Virginia Beach. Born and raised. It's one of those places that most people just go to for a week in the summer and don't think anybody actually lives in, but I do."

"No," you said, "no, I understand. I'm from the ocean too."

"Mara told me that," he said, smiling, "but I think I would have known anyway."

"How?" you said. You were not sure if this was flirting.

"You sound like saltwater," he said. "You look like waves."

You tried to smile at him, but your lips felt cracked and your skin tight and dry. His voice sounded no different, no different than if it were saying anything else. You were quiet and he was quiet, and into your silence came the movements of hands.

In the morning, you awaken into a strange sense of comfort, a feeling of composure that is full and palpable before you even open your eyes. It is not, either, the contentment of a brief naivety or forgetfulness—there is no crushing-in once you realize where you are. Instead, you simply wake up happy in your body and your mind, slowly identifying the objects of the world around you: the warmth of the air between your blanket and your skin, the smell of strangers and feet and coffee perking, and, last of all, the sound of rain on the roof and on the window. This, it occurs to you, is the reason for your mood; you have always slept most deeply to the sound of water.

You get up, searching around yourself for a clock; most of the blankets seem to be vacant, but outside the window is the pale-hazed light of early morning. You find the woman from the check-in counter setting up coffee urns in the breakfast room.

"The power's on for now," she says as you come in, "but this might be the last hot water we get."

"When did the rain start?" you ask, picking up a plastic-wrapped cheese danish and pulling it open, carefully, along the seams.

"Has it?" she says, threading and re-threading an urn lid until it slides into place. "I stopped looking at the windows. Hours maybe."

"Where is everyone else?" you ask. You break off a piece of the danish and put it in your mouth. It is sweet and oily and tastes artificial, but you feel your stomach churn with a kind of deep enjoyment. You realize that you ate nothing on your long drive the day before, driven as you were. You eat quickly, and when you are done, you pick up a poppy-seed muffin and eat that too.

"Scattered, I think," she says. You do not answer because your mouth is full of bright yellow crumbs, the fat coating your tongue, sticking to your teeth. She looks up at you for the first time and smiles as if she is happy to find it is you she is speaking to. "A few left, but most are still here. Around," she says, waving an arm, distracted.

You watch her for a moment as she moves from the urns to the tables that line the walls, laying out paper-lined baskets of napkins, plastic forks, and, at the end of the row, Andes mints. Her movements are clean and serious in a way that appeals to you. You notice her hands, long-palmed and tawny brown, flicking crumbs to the floor and smoothing the tablecloth while her eyes go on ahead, scanning the room for the next piece of work to be done.

"Can I help you with anything?" you say as you swallow the last of the muffin, prodding with your tongue for lost or captured poppy seeds.

She stops working for a moment to look you over, lips pursed, as if you were a problem to be solved.

"What would you like to do?" she says.

You shrug your shoulders, taken aback. "I could put out the rest of the danishes," you say, pointing to a half-filled box tucked under the table. There are plenty of danishes out already, neatly arranged on a silver-colored platter, but you do not know what else to say; you were only being friendly.

"Sure," she says, "whatever you like." She flips her black hair behind her ears, and the jerk of her head is quick, sharp. You wonder if you have offended her somehow—intruded upon her efforts. But then she smiles and turns back to her own work, and you think maybe you didn't see anything in her face at all. You find a second tray sitting behind the box and begin to load it with the pastries, trying to imitate her arrangement; you do not know what might matter to her.

"Are you alone here?" you say after a while. She does not respond right away, and you think maybe she has misunderstood you. "I mean, are there any other employees?"

"No," she says then, leaning over the table and straightening an edge. "I am alone here."

"I'm sorry," you say, but she stands up straight, shrugs her shoulders, and claps her hands together as if to clean them of some unseen dirt.

"I thought someone might come back this morning. There might still be time before the roads go." She smiles widely, chuckles deep in her throat. "I doubt it though. What kind of fool goes to work when the world is ending?"

"It's just rain," you say.

"Yes," she says. "I'm sorry. I wasn't trying to scare you."

You work for a little while longer, but then the tray is piled too high and looks ridiculous, as if you've all been invited to some ludicrous feast rather than a shelter in a storm. Still, you do not want to leave this room and this woman, and so you sit down at one of the little breakfast tables and watch her. You try to appear as if you are staring out the window—as if you are mired in the decisions you have not even begun to approach.

"How long have you been here?" you say when she passes close to you. It is no longer clear to you what work she is doing, in all her bustling about, and you wonder if she, too, is stalling.

"All my life," she says, a high note of surprise in her voice, as if it should have been obvious. "I was born here." Perhaps you look at her strangely, because she pauses on your face. "You mean just now," she says, "just since the storm. Two days, about. I didn't really mean to stay, but we saw what was coming on the news, and everyone just started to take off for home or, you know, to stay with people they thought would be out of range, and I didn't have anywhere like that to go, so I thought I'd stay through the end of my shift, at least. I don't have a TV at home, so I thought I could just stay and keep an eye on the news. Then everyone was gone, all my coworkers and all the guests, and it was just so quiet and eerie. I lingered. There wasn't any reason to go. Then, yesterday afternoon, people started arriving, people who were running away from it, and I thought, 'Well, why not just stay? Why not just make a use of myself?'"

"I didn't hear anything about all this," you say. "No one knew anything was going on."

"They didn't know for sure that it was coming here," she says, nodding her head. She is still for the first time since you've come in; you can really look at her now. She is older than you thought at first, closer to your mother's age than your own. "But it was so frightening, what happened up north."

"How bad is it?" you say, and you are going to tell her that you are from there, that you have left everything there, but when you hear your own voice, cracked and warbling, you know that she has guessed already.

"I can't tell you, honey," she says, her hand passing over yours so softly that you are not sure you have felt it at all. "I don't think anyone can tell you."

In the morning, the two of you walked from his truck, parked under the trees in an old horse pasture, to a diner in the spot where the little roads met the highway. When you began walking, you didn't know where you were going. The light came in through the windows of the truck the color of butter, and it looked so warm to you there, curled up tight against him, muscles sore from metal springs inside the cot, which seemed to have grown harder in the night. You crawled out without waking him, extracting yourself from a too-thick pile of sheets and down, and stood outside, leaning against the wheel well, breathing deep. It was a cold morning after all, and the grass was wet around your ankles. When he came out at last, he brought a blanket and draped it over your shoulders. You started walking just so he wouldn't try to drive you back to the house, and because you liked the feeling of the heavy fabric swinging at your back.

You went along the crest of a hill, and the land below you and around was planted with winter rye and some long green grass (timothy grass, he told you). When the wind blew, each blade bent against its neighbor so that the whole world was in motion and the land looked like water, or like a flock of birds, frightened. You thought of the song you'd sung in elementary school, staring at the flag stapled to the classroom wall, and you really felt something then—waves of grain. You told him that the place you were from was all rock cliffs and water and you'd never seen the plains before, and he laughed and said that Pennsylvania wasn't the plains at all. The plains don't have hills, he said. You could have told him that these weren't hills. You could have said that Mount Hood was a hill, but you liked the way he had been so many places, and he seemed to like it too, so you didn't say that.

A mile or so from the truck, the ground sloped down to meet the road, and when you saw the diner, you both realized how hungry you were. Before you went inside, he took the blanket from around your shoulders, folded it carefully into a square, and placed it beneath some bushes. The sun was warm now. Something in the exactitude of this motion amused you, and you chose a booth where you could see the green corner of fabric peeking out from its hiding place. You said you didn't want anyone to steal it.

Sometime while you were eating, his friend in Connecticut called, asking where he was, and you knew he would leave. Until then, neither of you could have been sure. He offered to drive you back to your sister's, but you refused, saying you could walk from there, getting it over with. Still, when you left him, he held the blanket draped across both of his arms, and when he kissed you the fabric wrapped around your torso once again, and on it you still smelled the scent of your bodies mingled, and he carried that with him when he went.

Later the others emerge, trickling out from rooms or from the makeshift dormitories that have sprung up in the upstairs halls. Whole families have slept in single beds. They are wide-eyed and harrowed. One woman had a room to herself—a young, pretty woman—and when this is discovered there is considerable anger. She is confronted, and cries. The day passes in blank comfort. The hours feel empty and quick. Around you, the others swap stories and form plans, but you make no friends and do nothing you will remember afterwards. You rest.

In the afternoon, a group of ten or eleven goes out to investigate the conditions on the road. They come back with mixed assurances. "It sure as hell looks passable to me," their leader says, "but there's no one out there—not a soul for miles in either direction. My guess is that it's a wash-out all around, but unless the news comes back on, we'd need someone to drive out and check."

There is a quiet after this. No one jumps to volunteer. You think of offering yourself; you do not share their sense of safety in this place or their fear of what is beyond. Still, you stay silent. You have no desire to make yourself noticeable here. If you go, you will not come back, but you have not yet decided to go. You feel time stretching towards something irrevocable, and you think you can still turn away. You think of driving back home through the water. You think of staying here and growing ghostlike.

"How far would we have to go?" a man asks. He is young and looks delicate in his glasses, his too-big sweater. A little blonde girl is playing around his feet. "Do we have any idea how far out the blockage could be, if there is one?"

"We don't even know what direction the storm is coming from," says the leader, "not for sure. No. We really know nothing."

"Is there really any point in sticking together?" says the young man. "Do we really help each other at all?"

The leader looks at him with an expression of dumbfounded contempt, and you are glad that you have stayed silent. You too would as soon be alone. You do not see that this burden would be lightened by sharing.

The woman from the check-in desk has been crossing off items on some sort of inventory list and seems not to have been listening at all, but she bobs her head up into the silence of their standoff and says, "There's no time limit. You can always come back. I'll stay until I know I everyone is safe."

You look into the serene determination of her face and think that maybe she is happier here than anyone.

You remember something Johnny told you, one day when you were lying together in your bed—it must have been the last day before he left. He was telling you stories about the Buddhists he had met in Nepal.

"There's a vow some of them take," he said, and the sunlight was all over him, "where they promise that they will not gain enlightenment until every other living soul in the world has gone before them."

"That's so beautiful," you said, reaching your hands around him, trying to find the warm places between planes of skin.

"No," he said, "it's insane. More than one of them has taken the vow."

"How will you possibly know that we're safe?" you say to the woman, but she only shrugs and smiles beatifically. You think that she will know as well as anyone. You think that she will know before you. The leader is not so easily reassured, and he shakes his head.

"Let's just get back to the topic at hand," he says.

You are standing near the back of the room, and you find it easy to slip away then, down one of the long halls of rooms lit too dimly with an endless parade of identical, cheaply antiqued lamps. You find a door left open and go inside. Clothes are thrown around the floor, men's and children's mixed, dresses and jackets entwining in piles that you realize, after a moment's inspection, looked slept-on. Someone has made the bed, though their work was sloppy and confounded by the many layers of stiff hotel linen. You lie down on your back and stare up into the cottage-cheese textured ceiling, staring so hard that your peripheral vision begins to melt and distort, and you feel engulfed by it, this plane of white sameness, this limit. You realize now that you have been waiting for something: some crisis to make your path clear. You think you should probably just go, ignore the warnings and the worried attempts to make a community of you. What good is it to stay? Yet some sort of malaise has overtaken you, an acquiescence. You can no longer imagine the difference between staying still and moving. You pull your phone from your pocket and dial, not hoping, exactly, but performing the actions nevertheless. It rings.

"Hello?" he says, and his voice is familiar and sweet, so clear and strong that you are afraid to speak, afraid to break the connection with your voice. "Shit," he says. "Jane, are you there?"

"I'm here," you say, and find that there are tears on your cheeks, fat and over-welling, constricting your throat and causing your nose to run. Wiping your face on the pillow, you feel ashamed not to have realized how much you missed him—the sound of him, the presence of his voice, the remembered touch of his skin to your skin, his wide, lined face, and the feeling of his eyes taking you in. You feel filled up with his voice, buoyed up by it. You want your journey to be over. "I'm fine," you say, "everything's fine."

He breathes strangely, a sigh, maybe, but short and choked-up somewhere within his body. You think that maybe he is crying too, but this is a different sound, something sharper.

"Jane," he says, "this is so scary."

"I know," you say. "I know, but I think I can just keep driving east. I don't think it's so bad yet. I just want to get to you. Everything else I can work out afterwards. I won't even think about it. I'm not going to worry about anything until I'm with you."

"I want to see you too, babe," he says, but there is a trailing-off in his voice—a something-else. You force yourself not to notice this.

"I think my father called me," you say.

"How'd he get your new number?" he says, and the strange note in his voice has disappeared, pushed out by a thrilling, protective rage.

"I have no idea," you say. "I don't know for sure it was him. The connection was bad. But..."

"You are sure," he says.

"Yes," you say. "I am sure."

He is quiet then—a pleasant, heavy silence.

"Well," he says at last, "it doesn't matter. I'm sure you're the least of his concerns now."

"What do you mean by that?" you say, and you think you know, but you will make someone tell you. He breathes in deep—you don't hear it but know he does it anyway—not having expected to be the bearer of this bad news. You think he is wondering how this fell to him, when he took up the burden of being dearest to you, the next of kin.

"Oregon is in bad shape right now, Janie. The whole Northwest got it."

"How bad is bad?" you say, determined.

"Underwater," he says. There is no crack in his voice, no hesitation, and, once again, you imagine his hand on the phone, the touch of his lips as he speaks. "From Vancouver to San Francisco. No one told you?"

"I've been alone," you say.

"There was some warning. A few hours. Plenty of people got out."

You do not reply, because you both know how little hope there is that anyone would have told him, alone in that cheap apartment by the highway, the television never turned on, maybe broken. He saw no one. You do not know what you hope for.

"People were still evacuating late yesterday afternoon. When did he call you?"

"Yesterday afternoon," you say. "Late yesterday afternoon."

He is quiet again. There is a feeling coming up in you—a new pain. Homesickness, you name it, homelessness.

"Just keep driving, Jane," he says, his voice rising as if yelling past some noise. "It's still moving inland. They don't know how far it will go. The safest thing is to just keep driving."

"The ocean?" you say. "Is it the ocean?"

"And the rain. The rivers."

"It can't come this far. I'm in the desert."

"It's too flat there. If the rain comes…"

You can hear the rain pounding at the windows and you wonder, in the pause, whether he could possibly hear it too.

"How far inland?" you say.

"I heard the Sierras. I heard it's getting serious there now."

"My mother," you say. "My mother too."

"Nothing is for sure, Jane. Just get in the car and get here safe."

You say that you will, that you love him, and that everything is going to be fine as soon as you're together, but as you lie there, the phone dropped beside you, an empty container for his voice, you think that he is wrong: some things are certainly, terribly, for sure.

You returned when the sun was high and hot to find Mara lying on the couch, her head resting on her arms. She sat up when you opened the door and said "Jane?" in a way that scared you; she sounded panicked, confused.

"I'm here," you said. "What's wrong?"

She leaned back down, running a hand through her hair.

"Nothing," she said. "I was just sleeping, I guess. Where were you? I was worried."

"I'm sorry," you said, coming to sit beside her. She lifted her head and put it in your lap. You let your fingers wrap into her hair, but this felt awkward and forced, and so you stopped and sat very still.

"I don't feel well," she said. "I think I overdid it last night."

"Me too," you said, though this was not exactly what you felt. "I think everyone did."

"Did you go somewhere with Johnny?" she asked, and after a moment you said that yes, you had. She breathed in, then out. She squirmed her body a little against yours, rubbing her face against your leg.

"I wish you wouldn't, Jane," she said. You tried, but you had nothing to say to that at all. "I'm sorry," she said, looking up into your face and trying to catch your eyes. "I'm not trying to tell you what to do, but there's so much drama with everyone here anyway. I just don't want things to get any more complicated. And Johnny...you know, he's..."

"What?" you said.

"One of them," she said, rolling onto her side and putting her back to you.

"They're your friends," you said.

"I like it here," she said, "but I'm not sure if I really fit in. Really, I mean. I think there is something about us that just doesn't."

"What do you mean, Mara?" you said. "You seem happy here."

"No, I am," she said quickly. "I don't know. It's just so nice here. Sometimes I think that everywhere I've ever been has been just so nice, and it's like I've never lived in the real world at all. And I know there is a real world out there, because of you, and then I just can't play along with the nice life everyone has here, and I get grumpy and mean, and then no one likes me."

"I'm sorry," you said. "I've never been great at having friends either."

"It's nothing like that," she said, reaching out a finger and swirling it in the dust on the floor. "They like me, I guess. They just don't come from where we come from, and they didn't have mom lying to them for all those years, so they think it's okay to be a little fake sometimes, and I just can't stand that."

"I think faking is a habit of well-adjusted adults."

"Sometimes they just seem so silly to me. They talk everything to death and act like growing some tomatoes in the back yard is going to start a revolution. They won't

[80]

even get a microwave, for God's sake. And in a way, I love it. It's all really sweet, and I feel...loved, I guess, but when it all comes down to it, they're just a bunch of rich kids playing at being something they aren't. Something that isn't even real anymore. I guess I shouldn't be, like, offended about it, but I really want to live in this real way, and I feel like they kind of mock that. Like they think that imposing hardship on themselves and putting themselves in shitty situations makes them more pure."

"Is that what shitty situations do?" you said. You were surprised by the way she looked at you then, steady and deep-eyed, as if every word you said was a message hurled across the space that had separated you.

"Maybe if they're real," she said. "I guess my life has been so easy too, compared to a lot of people. It just makes me nervous to think that maybe I'm somehow less genuine because of it, the same way those trust-fundy train hoppers are. Maybe I can't help it."

"Mara," you said, "why do you care so much about everything being real? What else would it even be?"

"I don't know," she said. "Home?"

You laughed, and she laughed too then, covering her face with her hand and glancing at you over the top. Her eyes stayed on you, and you wondered then if she'd meant it at all or if she'd said it all for your benefit. Was she wooing you? You thought of the black letters sketched into her date book, open on the car seat when you'd sat down, "Call Mom about visiting!" And you wondered.

"So, with Johnny," she said. "Please don't be upset with me. Just be careful. He's got a type."

"Which is?" you said, and even as you kept your voice cool, you knew she could feel your heart speeding up.

"He likes girls who are damaged."

You were amazed how hard this hit you. You had not realized you felt so much, already. You sat for a long time with your head tilted back, staring at the ceiling, as if this could fool her.

"I'm sorry, Jane," she whispered, reaching out her hand to touch your cheek, but you did not answer because you could not.

"All right," you said when you looked back down at her. "All right," and this time your voice was stronger. "He'll like me just fine then."

She looked at you for a little longer, eyes big and lips tight, pouting, her hair falling like a halo around her, like a child's drawing of the sun.

"Jane," she said, "Dad called."

You flew back home the next morning. Mara was upset. In the car on the way to the airport, she kept saying that she wasn't like your mother. She said she wanted you to stay, said that she wasn't afraid of him. But he had threatened her when she'd said you weren't there, and she cried when she repeated the things he had said, though she tried not *to. You saw that there was no point in letting her interject herself between the two of you. You would not let her save you the way she wanted to, and so she was disappointed in you, as much as she tried to cloak it in concern. "I just don't understand," she said, but you did. She'd dreamed up a story in which she delivered you from your father, and you redeemed her of your mother, and the two of you went on together, serious, formidable, and true. But you weren't what she'd expected. You didn't have any of the answers she wanted. You didn't know very much about the world at all. Then you'd gone and run off with Johnny, discovering him when you were supposed to be falling for her, and here you went cutting the whole story short, collapsing the exposition into the climax into the sad and sudden ending. No wonder she was angry. You knew she would not call again—not soon.*

You got off the plane in Portland, and you saw him before he saw you. You saw him before he turned, and you saw him before you noticed the dark bags under his eyes, their red rims, and before you realized how three days had drawn new lines into his face. You saw him before he came and placed his hand so lightly on your shoulder that you had to turn your head and look to be sure it was there, and before he brushed his lips against your cheek and rested there for just a moment, ear to ear. You saw him before he carried your bags for you, before he took you out and spent too much on dinner in the city, before he drove you back to a house that had been scrubbed cleaner than you had ever seen it, with all its leaks fixed and creaks oiled. You saw him before he stood wiping his eyes in your doorway, saying goodnight. Before all that, you saw him, and you felt something new: a total anger, a bone-wrath that made your throat go dry and your fingers cut into the palms of your hands. And that is what would save you.

The woman from the desk sees you gathering your things from the lobby floor, and though she does not approach you, you see the interest in her eyes. She recognizes of the change in you. She seems to see your knowledge. Most of the others have gone out in a group to explore the roads, splitting to the east and the west, searching for signals, probing into impassability. The children and the old people are sitting on the lawn, watching for some predetermined signs, being made to feel useful.

"Are you going?" she says, her voice so soft you are not sure she even means for you to hear or wants you to answer.

"I talked to my boyfriend," you say, "in the East. He says the flooding could come here too. It would be safest to get away while we can."

"I'll tell the others," she says.

"Do you think they'll be back soon?" you say, looking out the window to where the children are playing, drenched and pale-cheeked but splashing their shoes in the puddles that were potholes, charging between the new archipelagoes of the sandlot yard. "I don't think you should wait very long."

She smiles at you, sweet and distant, as if you amuse her.

"As long as need be," she says.

It strikes you then, what you have been seeing in that kind, familiar face of hers, and you can now name the thing that has drawn you to her quiet and her peace: it is lunacy. It is the fascinating lunacy of those people you always see on the news, hammering two-by-fours across the windows and saying, "This is my home, and I'm not going to leave it." It is the madness of the noble sea captains in weepy old movies, going down with the ship. Maybe the two aren't so different—you would be hard-pressed to say which she more nearly resembled, standing tall and straight behind the desk, her eyes fixed somewhere in the center of your head, looking through and beyond, and smiling like it was some big secret, this futile self-destruction. You think for a moment of taking her by the shoulders and shaking the smugness right out, saying, "I lived on a sinking ship for years, and there wasn't one brave part about it. Disaster is the easiest thing in the world," but you don't of course, because how could you? You stand up so that she will see you, a few inches taller, and you ask her what difference it could make if she stayed.

"People find other homes," you say. "There's nothing special about this place."

"It's not about that," she says. "It's not about this place. It's the principle that matters, and this just happens to be where I can make my stand."

"You're crazy," you say. "Everyone is going to leave, and you are going to be here by yourself. No one is going to come here. You will not be helping anyone."

She smiles at you again, and it makes you furious.

"Does it mean any less if I do it alone?" she asks, and though you don't even know what she means, you say, "Yes," and finish picking up your things without saying another word. As you make your way to the car, you consider telling the old women huddled there under the eaves of the roof to gather their families and go, but you know that she will be good to her word and will warn them. She'll drive them away if she has to, jealous of her martyrdom.

7

Later, you pull off onto a side road, sheltered by a rock wall and sure that you will not be noticed if one of the cars from the hotel passes by on the highway. The water is pouring down in droplets from the east and in a heavy cascade from the west. It has coursed down the ruined cliff face, picking up polished, scorched rocks and muddy sand on its descent. The ground around you has turned sticky and raw, but the weather now neither surprises nor upsets you. You think for a moment that you are accepting, becoming used to, but this is quickly overtaken by the knowledge that you are only sunk into the midst. You get out of the car and sit on the hood, liking, at first, the feeling of the rain soaking through to your scalp and running like cold fingers along the furrows of your hair. Soon, though, the water has soaked through your sweater, and you feel heavy and chilled. You are too aware of your body, swaddled and confined in the sodden cloth, ill-fitting and uncomfortable. You had thought that you were going to cry—that was, as far as you had thought about it at all, the reason you had stopped driving—but now you no longer feel the desire. Something within you has flattened in response to the low hang of the sky and the blurred gray of the distant horizon. Turning slowly, you find a vast sameness, an anyplace with all its particulars obscured and transformed by the pall of the rain. You remind yourself which direction you've come from, feeling the ease with which you could be lost. This, you think, is a comfort; this is what it means to be rid of your entanglements.

It is dusk, and the light has grown into its dying density. Even through the thick curtain of the rain, the air—the particles of air, the body of the light itself—seems filled up, wrapped tightly around a core of incandescence: a golden, purple, blue, a red, a color that is unimaginable except in its form, draped through the substance of the sky. This is your favorite time of day. *You have spent hours trying to put words to the feeling that you have taught yourself for this time, when you would sit on the front porch, just home from work and not yet gone inside, or with dinner resting beside the stove, too hot to touch. The sun would be gone, but the light would remain, a bright fog resting on the ocean. It would be very quiet, and the feeling was something like being at home in the world, or being at home and greeting the world as an expected visitor, a friend you make no fuss about. The sky would be like a blanket and the air like the touch of a beloved animal's fur, but the water would be something you could never, never put a single word to. There your metaphor making would break down, and you would sit quiet and thoughtless until it was dark, or you were hungry, or your father would call out to see if that was you out there. You were always very happy in these moments, when you caught them.*

The light here is not so different from the light of home, though there is an unfamiliar diffusion, a softness around the objects it touches. The sky is higher and the trees not quite right—too few and too small, too bare—you miss the pines. The sound of the rain is familiar: a comforting echo of the ocean. You could close your eyes and be lost, could open them to find yourself just outside your door on any number of chill autumn evenings. But you will not; the known world is gone, replaced by this other place, this simulacrum. You wonder if the world will always be a translation for you now—if you will know it only through equivalencies and comparisons, love it only by the words you created to fit the contours of another place.

You spent months wanting Johnny, after you returned from Pennsylvania, after your father was gone. You spent months cultivating your image of him, encouraging it to grow into the empty spaces your family had left, plowed under and uprooted. At night, you kept him on the phone too long, knowing that his midnight meant, for you, another three hours of sitting up, reading in your empty house with the sound of the tide moving in, and feeling every time you looked up that the walls had moved out wider, that soon you would lose them altogether. Sometimes you would call him again, full of apologies once you heard how patient he sounded, how tired. You needed his voice to root you back into yourself and to assure you that you still had that, at least, after all you'd jettisoned. Always you asked him to come, and always he said he wanted to and said he would.

Then, finally, he came, and it was all different than you'd expected or wanted, and nothing you did could bite back the knowledge of something being broken in you, some warmth chilled. By the time Johnny had been in your house for two days, you hated him. He was beastly—a beast, a stupid animal rummaging, filthy-snouted, bloody-clawed, and sacrilegious. In your bed the first night it had felt like rutting, like his hands left their scent on your skin—he'd finished howling. Soon everything smelled like him, like the animal musk of his thick hairs and half-dried sweat; his fingerprints smudged the banisters and the windows. The air that had passed through him went greasy—humid and choked. You'd warned him—said your house was a beautiful, frozen place by the sea: an ice palace. But all he'd heard was "fairy tale" and not "careful," and so his stay was a cacophony of cracking and crushing and dripping that he seemed not to hear at all.

Worst of all, he began to intuit. His clumsy occupation of your life had overturned the flowerpots and sent the mice scurrying for the corners. There were revelations, and you saw him absorb them with a look of solemn concern that made you turn glib and mocking.

"Your father…" he'd say, or, "How long?" but you'd only stare him down with your eyes halfway rolled like you were looking over top of glasses, and he'd never have the strength to ask further.

For the first time in a long while, the house felt full—of them as much as of him. He'd brought the whole sorry bunch jostling out of the woodwork—the complications and the exclamations, the things that could not be worked around, and that was fine because you knew they'd drive him off. There simply wasn't space enough. He must have felt eyes on him; he wanted to get out. He kept asking to go hiking or swimming or to drive into town. Mostly you obliged him because you felt caged up with him there anyway, but you and your home were like sisters, and he didn't have the sense to see that he was insulting you both. Finally, he asked if you wanted to go camp out for the night, and you'd had enough.

"In the yard?" you asked. "Like eight year olds? Should I call my mom to bring us snacks?"

It was the first time he was ever really angry with you. You told yourself that he looked pitiful out there alone, staking his tent into the loose sand of the cove where he thought you could not see him. You could see him, from the top of the house, where you'd always liked to hide, and where your father said you shouldn't go because it was bad for the roof.

He'd made a big show of driving away, and for a while you'd really believed he was going. You'd spent an hour sitting in the same chair you'd been in when he left, reading a book with a luxurious calm, just in case he came back and needed a further demonstration of your coolness. When you were sure he was gone, you got up and went to the kitchen to make dinner, but found yourself drifting around the house instead, trying to find the feeling of the place again and butting up against the ghostly presence of his departure. As always when you felt something closing in on you, you made your way to the roof, and there you spotted the red dot of his truck not even half a mile away and laughed out loud in a crude and unexpected burst of real disdain.

Still, you watched him until it got dark, trying to decipher the distant movements of his body, hardly distinguishable from the movements of all other things or the distortions of air or light or eyes. You liked him better when you only thought of his body moving in the rough and ordinary motions of nest making. You liked the way he moved—had liked, in each of your brief encounters, to find him in the moments when he felt unwatched. You realized that in observing only his actions—clearing a place and pitching a tent, gathering wood to make a small, hot fire—you were seeing a man quite different from the other—simultaneous—man, the one with the pouting and the moods, the spitefulness, and the arrogant belief that you would come out there after him. The same actions, the making of camp and food, when ascribed to this man, were repellent to you, petty and pitiful. Worst of all, this man implicated you—made you the subject of his little performance. You felt sullied and, still, drawn in. It was cheap and thrilling to know he was thinking of you even as the body went about its work—a rich, red clot in its austerity. You imagined both men at once, and somehow their shared form seemed only incidental to their obvious inequality. You wanted to go to the body and to go reject the man all over again—which is to say you wanted to go to where he was.

When it was too dark to see him anymore, you went back inside and sat in the kitchen drinking a glass of wine. You'd let the bottle sit open too long, and it had turned *sharp and animal tasting. You didn't mind this; it felt like company. Your father had been gone for ten weeks, and you'd begun to feel a permanent adjustment to his absence. The air and water seemed to be filling up the spaces he had occupied, and so you believed he was really gone, or that, if he returned, it would be different.*

You had now begun to discover, after years of wanting only to be left alone, that you were no good at it. You'd not been unprepared to live by yourself, but you'd expected to find something within you—some main beam, some solid core—that would keep you through your loneliness. You'd expected that some long-stifled vividness would be set loose in you. Instead, you had found a vast vapidity, an inward sea of tides and turnings, all bewilderingly moonless and unmoored. You hardly knew how you spent your days. After a week, maybe, or only an hours' stretch without a human voice to intrude upon your silence, you became dull and panicked. You paced the walls of your world in search of the escape route that had eluded you the time before and the time before and before and before.

Johnny—the promise of Johnny when he was still far away—had made your solitude feel reasonable to you, normal even. The absent lover was a nameable problem. Someday he would come. Not so for the rest of the fairy-tale cast of absentees and phantasmal presences. They were anything but simple, anything but solvable: the monstrous father with his returns and regenerations (seven-headed like the hydra); the wicked mother and her enchanted, chosen thrall; even the churning waters of the Pacific played their part in the tale—sometimes they came to your window at night and sang. There had been so much of the monstrous in your upbringing that only the most ordinary life could keep it on its chain. Solitude only twisted your world into the wilder shapes of the unconscious and the allegorical. Johnny had been just a regular-enough man who had believed you were a regular-enough woman, and this had made your existence seem suddenly approachable and plain. Even loneliness seemed with him just a "fact of life"—that wonderful phrase which took in everything and wore it down to mere cranky benignity. He'd been an anchor. He'd made you feel still.

With the possibility settling on you of another depopulation, you felt yourself turning puppyish and afraid. You were still angry, but even your anger seemed ridiculous and outsized—the little dog snapping at the Doberman's heels. You didn't want him to come back, and you certainly didn't want to go to him, but you wanted him to stay put, to stay promised—and you knew he would not, not for very long. You'd hardly be the first woman to choose the almost-right thing, the necessary facsimile of the desire. You poured yourself another glass because you could make him wait, at least, and could perhaps still outwait him. The wine had made your throat feel soft and your feet heavy— perhaps you would sleep. The temperature outside was dropping and the house had begun to groan your daily lullaby.

You remember the letter you have carried from The Pauline and feel ashamed of the self who took it. The idea has become ridiculous to you—

the vanity of believing you could make a story of her, could shape her into a better reflection of your own. You push yourself off the hood of the car and open the door, rummaging through the trash that has accumulated under the passenger seat until you feel its sharp, hardened edges against your fingers. You hold it for a while, not sure what you mean to do, meditating on the name Pauline as if it held the answer to whatever question you are asking or groping towards asking. It is silent, and so you insert your index finger underneath the seal and pull slowly down the paper's slope. You shake the letter out and read it, the movement of your eyes only a little faster than the disintegration of the paper, and sometimes not fast enough. The signature has emptied into rivulets, and before you are sure what you've read, the blue of "Love, Mattie" or maybe "Lovingly, Mandy" or perhaps even "Love, Daddy"—you can't rule it out—has become embedded into the lines of your palms, has soaked into indecipherability.

He was already sleeping when you unzipped the tent flap and climbed in, awkward and fumbling in the darkness and the small space. He was breathing big, oblivious breaths through his open mouth and didn't even half-wake at your entrance. He didn't even roll out of your way as you jostled his arms and legs, trying to find a space to lie down that his body hadn't already claimed. This offended you. You'd imagined him sleepless.

Of course, you had slept too—on the couch downstairs, feeling out-of-sorts and indecisive and too jarred to go to bed. This had been the mistake that brought you here; you'd awoken in the density of the night, and there had been no moon, but the overhead light was still on, flooding the house in seventy-watt obscenity. You had not known when it was, or where, and, in that moment of confusion, desire had gotten the best of you. You'd thought of his body, sunk down into the fine sand of the cove, awake in the cold, and waiting.

There had been a thrill in giving up that had lasted you through awakening and dressing, and almost through the chilled stumble down the bluff to the water, but the calf-aching slog through the half mile of deep sand had worn away the last of your enthusiasm. You had gone on only because it seemed too far to go back. Now, curled uncomfortably in the darkness beside his heavy, unconscious form, you felt foolish. You considered leaving but were stopped by the possibility that he might remember your coming in the morning and realize how ridiculous you'd been. Disappointment had added another smothering layer to your exhaustion, and though your teeth chattered with something that wasn't only the cold, and though you felt as if sleep were something you'd made up a long time ago, you were under before the first light began to make its gray arrival out over the hills.

Johnny woke you with a hand on your shoulder—not quite rough—but you lost this chance. There was something he would have said to you if you had not pretended to sleep a few seconds longer, if you had not pulled the edge of his unzipped sleeping bag more tightly around your shoulders. He left the tent without saying anything. You had not considered the possibility that he did not want to be followed. You stayed put for a while, wrapped in the blanket he had abandoned and feeling something warm and heavy drifting over your mind until you were not thinking or feeling anything at all. This was something you had always known how to do. It felt like sleeping, but stretched out longer and slower, made savorable. You had always wondered how long you could keep up in this state—hours probably, maybe years—but had never tried to test yourself. Something always brought you back, and you let it, knowing that the longer you stayed away the more difficult the return. These were small indulgences, but little doses of un-being could lead to harder stuff if you let them.

Outside the tent—when you finally emerged, still hazy and blank, locked in an unwilling struggle to consciousness—Johnny was lying in the sand just beyond where the water reached with the outside edge of the best waves. The sand there was neither wet nor dry, but dense and giving as moss. He appeared to be asleep, and this caught you in a way you had not expected or prepared for. Something inside you clenched painfully at the thought that he had not wanted even to sleep beside you. And at something else— something about his body in the sand, the intersection of earth and skin, which was a more pure loss, a deeper alienation.

You went and sat beside him, not quite touching his hand with yours, digging your nails down into the sand and drawing them up again, dark and encrusted with salt. A wind was picking up over the water, whirling it, and you wondered if it would rain. The sky was overcast, but you guessed from the watermark that it must have been well past noon. The tide was going out, and a widening glitter appeared where the waves had retreated, studded with rocks and shells. You had meant to wake him, but now found that you couldn't. You felt will-less and vast, as if in your sleep you had grown and spread out across the cove and into the ocean. As the water pulled away, you found you wanted to swim, and so you stood carefully and stripped off your clothes, leaving them in a heap beside his body, a reduction, an effigy of yourself.

When you swam you liked to run into the water, fighting to keep your feet until the swell of the waves picked you up and turned you, dropping you on your belly or your back. Then you would dive down and swim hard, not looking back until you were sure you were out of sight of land, though you never were. Someday you would be, and you would float there for a long while, not knowing which way to go. You liked that the ocean was so much the same from edge to edge. You liked that, once inside it, you could be anywhere at all. It felt the same every day; though the temperature changed, and though sometimes there was wind, or sun, or rain, somehow it always greeted you in the same rough way. It wrapped around you, filling up your empty and negative spaces, it grasped at your ankles and your wrists, and it pulled you down by the tightening rope of your hair. You would fight back until you were free, kicking and jerking your limbs away, cutting through the body of the water with the strength of your arms until you were gasping and tensionless, out beyond the current. It was good to have something to fight back against. This was how you knew how much fight was in you.

You were surprised how strong you felt, despite the little sleep and the chill fog, and you wished for a moment that Johnny would awaken and see you. You thought you must look fine and hard. You thought this must be how you looked best. Still, you did not look back to see if he was watching, because you never looked back until you could not go farther forward. You had always wished that this was the way you lived your life onshore, but it was not. It was only the way you swam. The water gave way around your body, grabbing and tugging. Today it felt just a little softer and more familiar—indulgent even, like your father wrestling with you when you were very young, letting you win, pretending your chubby little arms had his big ones pinned. You had felt lonely, and you welcomed the touch of the water, though you worked as hard as ever to cast off its grip. Tender or not, it would sink you if it could.

When your lungs ached too much to fill, and your breath was like water overflowing a glass, you stopped swimming and slowly turned shoreward, contemplating the long, slow return. Johnny had awoken and was sitting in the sand, watching you. You wondered if he had really been asleep at all. The idea entered you as another heavy ache. You decided that you would not rush yourself in swimming back to him; you were too tired anyhow, even if you'd allowed yourself that display of undismayed longing. Still, you felt a nervous heartbeat peeking from behind the heavy rap of exertion. You felt sure he would rise and walk away at the last second, refusing to look back as you always looked back in such moments. Your quickness could stop him, but your arms felt like roots growing towards the water. They were immeasurably slow, slow like the time of un-human things to which time makes no alterations. Whenever your head rose above the water, you were amazed to find him still waiting—though you swore you wouldn't look—sitting so still and watching, though it took you ages to reach him.

"I hate it here," he said, just as the last wave had flowed back around your ankles, before you even decided if you would walk to him or past him. "You're a jerk when you're here."

You were going to say that who you were in this place was who you were completely, that no one had a gun to his head he didn't have to stay, that he didn't really know you at all, but you couldn't. Instead, you felt something perverse bubbling up into your throat, some traitorous excitement at his vehemence, his easy dismissal of the things you loved and which defined you. It was an opening cut into the limits of your life. It was the wild and unwieldy power of rejection, dangled before you on a string. It was simply rebellion: childish, necessary, and glorious in its blood-splattered primacy. He did not know you and would not notice if you transformed; you could betray and abandon and burn-to-dust the life you'd been raised into, and with his mere ignorance he would wipe it all clean. So when you said, "Where would you like me better?" he probably thought it was acquiescence, but it wasn't that at all. It had nothing to do with him at all.

When you are done reading, you set the paper on the car roof and let the rain tear into it, searching for something it would not reveal to you. The words were intimate enough, telling enough: there were plans and pipedreams, long-standing anxieties, problems, attempts to assuage, or reassure, or bully into acceptance. There was a life in it, a personhood, but whatever osmotic identification you had expected to take place had not. Your compulsive theft, your harboring of this artifact, had affected no change in the thing itself. It remained as impenetrable, as not you, as any other accounting of days and relations without the necessary key of the days that came before. You realize now how little you have been able to guess of this girl, of anyone you see only by their leavings, their actions, the visible tip which clears the surface of the past. You are not like her—this girl who stayed—and she is not the ghost who haunts your emptied house, your ruined home. She is not what you might, so easily, have been, any more than you are yourself that imagined woman who stayed in the house by the sea and lived some other life. You cannot probe the depths of her, the ends of her, for your own fortunes. You are free of her memories, to be mired in your own. You are free of her. You wipe the wet remnants of the paper off of the car and watch for only a moment as the blue ink swirls in the eddies of the ground. You get back in the car, turn on the heat as high as it will go, and find your way back to the road.

The plans were made over a day and a half spent curled in the slowly dishing bottom of the tent. They were wild, romantic plans, and they poured from the both of you like the unquestioned absurdities of sleep talk, forming an urgent world parallel to the one where you had lived. You would come to each other in an unknown place, in the center of the distance that had divided you; you would make any kind of life. It was a sort of game, the making of these confabulations, the layering on of details until the structure couldn't hold—the garish decoupage of your future. Still, you were not playing; you were quite serious. There was an agreement: the things you said would be made to come true. Having never rebelled before, you found yourself marvelously equipped for it. You had amassed so many possible lives.

The plan, after the last round of negotiations and escalating dares, was simple and alarming in its starkness: in a few months, when you had saved enough money or any money at all, you would set out from your former home with as much as you could squeeze into a station wagon and no more. Between the two of you, you would drive the length of the nation, and you would meet in the middle. You did not, then, know exactly where that middle was, but you had visions of a wide expanse that was in every way like the ocean, except for being land. You would live in the center of a wide-open place. That was all, really. You would have a life there. You might get married; you might as well. That was all—a place in the middle where you could see for a long way around.

On the second day of your planning, rains moved in and the rest of the world turned gray and inconsequential. Outside, everything went liquid, fog drenched, but inside, the little light was filtered through the red plastic of the walls, and your bodies glowed with the unnatural color, ruddy and bold. Neither of you wanted to go back to the house until the water seeped through the decaying seams of the tent and soaked your blankets. You didn't want to go back even then, afraid that the move would reveal you to yourself, would prove that you were a giddy and impractical child, a schoolgirl spreading gossip. You needn't have worried: a traverse had been accomplished. To scale your way back to where you'd started from would have taken more than you had left, and perhaps was not possible at all. From this new angle, every familiar thing looked strange; it felt as if you'd undergone a narrowing of the vision, a lengthening. Your senses functioned through a fish-eye lens, and the world around you touched you less. Everything was distant and illusionary—a mirage of memory like a haze on the horizon. You had decided to leave, and that was sufficient to sever the ties you had thought essential to your holding-together at all.

When Johnny left two days later, you found yourself desperately sad—not for the loss of him but for the loss of your home. The house had shrunk since his entrance, turning seedy and common with crumbs in the corners and a small, drizzly view of the sea. Your first, unconscious love of the place had broken, and, for the first time in your life, you felt displaced. You hated the thought of living out another month in the husk of your former limits. You thought of the hermit crabs that you loved to catch and cage as a child, a whole parade of them with names you could still remember, though they never lasted long. When they outgrew a shell, they'd leave it and find another, and it looked like they were leaving a part of themselves, but they were not. Awful little scavengers, they lived in the hollowed out bones of things that had died and rotted and been swept entirely away. You would work double shifts every day they would let you at the grocery, and still you would leave with barely enough money to make it even most of the way.

8

Things get worse. The images from the news begin to wash in all around you. When you stop for fuel, you find the station abandoned, five-gallon gas cans lined up by the pump, looked over by a homemade sign citing bible verses you do not know. You take as many of the cans as you can fit in the trunk, grab a handful of candy bars from the store, and pee in the eerie silence of the bathroom, where you lock the door, though you are quite alone. You want that protection still, though you want it from the quiet and the loneliness itself, not from the truckers and travelers who should rightly be congregated here, intimidating you with their noise and their obvious belonging in this place where you do not belong.

Mostly, you are not thinking of your father, but the thought of him is there nevertheless—the crackling sound of him straining through the phone. Those were, you believe, the last words you will ever hear from him—those collapsed, inarticulate sounds, your name—and you wonder if he knew it when he spoke them. *You know the room he would have called from; it bothers you to imagine him surrounded by that place, those things that were not his. You went there, to that awful room, a week before you left town. You went because to do so was satisfying the way picking a scab is satisfying, and the damage only gave you more to pick.*

The hotel was on the other side of town, away from the water and past the thin strip of tourist shops selling saltwater taffy and marked-up sweatshirts. Just five miles from the beach, but already the place was "inland"—unfashionable and deserted. The hotel was called The Catalina, which made you think of salad dressing, and there was a smell of vinegar in the air, of something spoiled. The walls were stucco, painted pink, and rooms were arranged in two levels around a central courtyard. Slabs of concrete formed stairs. You stood in the courtyard for a while, pretending to scan the numbers on the doors, but really just waiting, just a bit longer. Around you were potted plants—hardy, not wilting—and lawn chairs arranged in festive circles, as if some happy group had just broken up or moved along. There was rust on all the legs and on the hinges.

It was the kind of hotel people lived in; in the summertime there would have been a vacationing family, more or less tricked into this fleabag, their eyes betrayed and embarrassed at what they'd come to, and the children with sunburns and red eyes. Now it was almost winter, and so there was no one but a man sleeping on a bed with the door open and an old woman leaning against the banister at the bottom of the stairs, moving her mouth like it was full of peanut butter. She was silent, and you brushed past.

You had hoped that he would not be in when you arrived, but, of course, he was, and, of course, you had hoped for that too. You knocked lightly at the door, and for barely a second there was no corresponding noise from inside, and in that time something strange happened inside your chest—a missed beat, or an extra—and then his voice said, "Just a minute," and you felt it again.

He did not look surprised to see you, nor, exactly, pleased. He looked very tired. He looked as if he was making a great effort. You wondered, as you looked into his slack and expectant face, whether he was just mirroring your own expression or whether he, too, was worn out by you, by the unwieldy space between you. He stepped back from the doorway and gestured you inside.

The room was not dirty, only shabby. Still, you felt a creeping revulsion and did not want to sit anywhere or to touch anything for too long. The walls were paneled with light-colored fake wood, and you sensed a long-neglected nautical theme, now expressed only by a wicker loveseat draped with plastic fishing nets. You sat on that, balanced on the edge, and your father sat on the bed across from you. He folded his hands. He looked down.

"I can't stay," you said. "I'm on my way to work. I just wanted to see how it was."

"It's all right," he said, "as a temporary arrangement."

"Well, okay then," you said, standing up, angry that he tried to guilt you in that way, in that moment. You do not know what would have happened if he had been kinder, but you left, and you thought, for a time, that this would be the last thing you ever heard from him.

All around you, the desert looks shocked. The scorched and sandy earth has boiled up into a blood-red mud studded with stones, uprooted bunchgrass, and the little bodies of lizards and unnamable, eyeless creatures washed up from the ground. The rain has carved shallow, looping riverbeds into the dirt, and all of the world seems to be slipping into them as they combine and multiply. Nature itself seems somehow caught off-guard, though you know you are only projecting because you have seen no one else on this road with whom you can share your surprise, your mounting fear.

You have begun to hear a sound—a low whisper, a sweet growl. You cannot tell the distance or the source, though you have your suspicions. It is a sound on the very edge of hearing, and you find yourself compelled to hum or sing loud, to play the radio's static, to drown it out because, you tell yourself, the sound bothers you—it is a constant annoyance, it is driving you crazy. But really, it does not annoy you. It is familiar, almost soothing: the natural sound of the world existing around you. When you plug your fingers into your ears and make it stop, you do so not to escape its presence but only be sure that the source is still somewhere real, somewhere outside of yourself. You have lived so long with the sound of the ocean; you would be only a little surprised to find it so inescapable, carried in the sound of your blood flowing or hidden in the stream of your thoughts. You think that when you get to Johnny you will have him put his ear to yours, or to your chest, or to your belly, and you will tell him to listen because you echo like a conch shell.

For now, though, the noise seems to be purely present tense and external. You think, for a while, of turning back to find the shore of whatever it is that is lapping up behind you, but you quickly see how ridiculous a plan that is. You do not always find it easy to tell when you must run towards and when away. You are not as sure as you should be of the difference. You keep driving, and the noise waxes and wanes as the day goes on, slipping sometimes into silence and sometimes becoming loud enough that you expect to find the watery edge of the world waiting to swallow you around every curve. It is not until the nighttime—when you lie wrapped in your dirty clothes, squeezed between your suitcases, straining to hear the water getting close but detecting only the slow patter of the droplets and the last, lonely cries of the cicadas—that you understand the way the sound comes and goes: it is the tides.

Slipping into sleep, you remember a movie you watched as a kid, your father's favorite, or one that he knew would keep you quiet and enraptured long enough for him to do whatever it was he was doing. The movie was about an old woman who lived by the sea, like you, and who had lost someone—her husband, maybe, or her son—to drowning, and she always waited for him, but he did not come home. She had some keepsake of this man, and she treasured it, a sort of talisman against the sea. Then, one day, the sea came up into her house, and flooded the rooms, and took her treasure back away from her. There was more to the story, but this is what you remember. You knew even then that it was supposed to be scary to you, but it was not. Now you know you are falling asleep because you are not sure if you ever really saw this movie at all or if you are imagining it, because the house you remember is your house, with water wrapping around the doorframes like fingers and pulling itself into the rooms, lifting up the weight of bodies, and carrying them away.

In the morning, you notice something strange on the horizon, a shimmer like heat waves rising from blacktop. It is cold, though. Despite the rain having slowed, the clouds hang so low that their bottoms scrape across the rising wisps of fog so that the whole air is a single, damp mass. It is not heat you see rising but light—a sudden change in the reflective substance of the ground. The shimmer is behind you as you drive, but your eyes keep catching it in the rearview mirror, trying to ascertain if it has grown since the last time you glanced up from the road. Each time, in the blink-second before you feel the car begin to drift from the center of the road and into the softening, mudded-over curves, you assure yourself that it has.

You are not sure where you are anymore. The desert seems to be slowly filling in. The empty stretches of dirt and scrubby, brown grass are cluttered out and replaced by towering rock formations, imposing shapes that rise up all around you as you wind your way down into canyons where the fog has settled so neatly it looks like it's been leveled off with a knife. The rocks are deeply grooved with fingernail scrapes where they have been worn away by centuries of the wind bearing down—wiping the mouths of the earth. The rocks stand in shades of red, and pink, and a glowing white that frightens you when it appears out of the fog. In your mind, you hear the word sepulcher, stuck there like a fragment of a song.

You feel lonely in a way you have not felt since you were a child, sitting at the living room window and watching for your mother's green station wagon to fill the empty road. But your mother would be far away, and you would feel yourself beginning to cry like a creature clambering up out of your throat. You were undone by that absence.

Now you wish for Johnny; you try to remember the last moment of his presence and to feel again the warm press of his hand against your skin. The morning he last left you, you cried into his chest, saying, "It won't be the same when I can't feel you here." He shushed you and petted your hair back from where it had gotten tangled into your teeth and the cracks in your lips. "I'll call every day," he told you. "We'll talk more than when I'm here." But that hadn't been enough for you; you needed him bodily. You needed the simple reality of him to eddy around. You cannot remember the last place that he touched you, and this makes the miles ahead seem impossible.

Near to noon, the clouds roll up off the face of the sky, and you find that you are at the foot of a huge mountain, the name of which you do not know. This bothers you because you feel that you are moving not only into silence but also into inarticulateness; you have always known the names of things, at least. You have pulled into another small town, the streets narrow and close-packed, and all the buildings facing in towards the center—a circled wagons kind of place. Though you see no signs bearing the name of the town, you imagine they would say something like "The Miniature Metropolis!" or "An Oasis in the Desert!" It is a proud place—self-conscious—and you know it must have been a true hurt for the people who lived here to abandon it so totally. There is no sign of anyone left behind; the streetlights click from red to green in a mechanical calm uninterrupted by the rumble of traffic or voices. Every block or so, you see a house with boarded-up windows, but mostly they are just shut and darkened, not yet sunk into the terminal emptiness that precedes decay. You feel as if you are interrupting something—the unknowable wholeness of places without people. You enter with your noise and drive off a more perfect quiet. You can feel it there, crouching at the edges of your sight, waiting for you to leave.

At the outskirts of the town, you see signs for a highway—a large interstate that you know will take you across the Rockies and the rest of the way to Kansas. You try to remember what roads the newsman at the hotel had told you to avoid, where he said the flood had circled down into valleys, making unpredictable inroads and moats. You cannot recall if this road was on the list, and, even if you could, you would not be able to trust that days-old news. The road goes up, which is all you can hope for. *You have spent too much time moving down and diving into.*

Nearby to the highway entrance is a grocery store, and you stop here, knowing that you have been lucky, so far, to navigate these little roads and outpost towns as well as you have. From here on there will be no stopping and no straying from the path. The sliding door does not move as you approach it; unlike the owners of that ragged-edge-of-nowhere gas station, the people of this comfortable town have been slow to accept that they won't be coming back. You are not immune to that optimism, that unfaltering belief in the soundness of your world; you feel a real hesitation, a painful criminality, as you bring the tire iron out of your trunk and swing it hard against the glass, three times until the bottom pane is clear enough for you to duck through. The wail of the alarm makes your jaws water, but you tell yourself not to run, and you do not.

As you'd suspected, the lights have been turned off but the freezers left on. You open a box of plastic spoons and sit with your back against the shelves, sampling the ice creams and sucking on the frozen berries, cracking them in your teeth. You do everything you might have imagined you would. You try to deny yourself any pleasure in your thefts, but as you wander up and down the aisles, opening boxes and pouring their contents into bags to make room for more, more than you could possibly need, you feel a gleeful happiness, a sense of having gotten your due, of conquest over this drowned world.

When you are done, the car is an architectural glory, supplies stuffed tight in hanging towers that would topple if anything moved—if anything could. You think of how proud Johnny will be when he sees your haul—when he sees how fit you are for making a world. But when you notice that your phone, reception-less since you'd left the hotel, has a single, wavering bar, it isn't him you call.

"Oh my God, Jane," she says. "I can't believe I'm talking to you. Tell me you're all right."

"I'm all right," you say. She begins to sob, and you are surprised by this—always surprised by the quick pain of others. You sit silent through the snot-bubbling sounds, the rustle of a sleeve wiping across the phone. She tries to speak but can't get the words out, and you want to help her, to fill the line with your voice. "I'm not sure if my reception will last," you say. "If I lose you, just know that I'm okay."

"Who's with you?" she says. It takes you a moment to realize what she's asking, and another to hear the terror in the question.

"I'm alone," you say. You wait for another sob, but there isn't one. "Mara?" you say, thinking the line has gone dead, but she says, "I'm here," in a voice that is small and strange to you, a voice that is welling up from somewhere. "I think I'm in Utah," you say. "Maybe Colorado. I'm going to Kansas to be with Johnny. I saw Mom the day the flood started, but I don't know where she is now. They were listening to the radio. They could have found out in time." You are talking fast, hoping the connection will hold. You feel a compulsion to report to her, to have her know all that you do, all that you have done.

"I don't understand," she says. "You were with Mom?"

"Yes," you say. "I was with her. I want to tell you everything, but I'm afraid the phone is going to die. I want you to know that I'm okay and that I don't know about Mom, but I think she and Steve had enough time to get out."

"But why wouldn't they call me? They would have been able to call, if you can."

"I don't know," you say. "I don't think anyone knows very much. There hasn't been any radio since it started, hardly any TV. It's like the whole world has emptied out. I'm in this town, and there's no one here. It's like I'm the last woman on earth. Are you really still out there?"

"I am," she says. "Way the fuck out here and I can't stand it. I'd rather be with you. I want to be with Mom. Will you come here, Jane? I want to see you. I'm so fucking alone now."

She is crying again, and something glib and cruel comes dangerously close to the surface of your mind, but you push it back down and drown it before it speaks.

"As fast as I can. Just let me get to Kansas safe, and then we'll figure something out. It's all getting better now. You're not alone."

"What's in Kansas? Is it safe there?"

"I don't know," you say.

The familiar cracking has begun to cloud the connection, rising and falling with the sounds of her breath.

"This is going to break off," you say.

"Jane," she says, "don't hang up."

"I'm not," you say, but you don't think she hears you.

"What about Dad?" she says, and you know it is the question she has been trying to ask all along, the thing that was building up behind her sobs, pushed through at the last moment.

The phone does not go dead, not right away, but you wait it out.

9

You no longer know how long you have been driving, though you know that you have slept, maybe once, or maybe twice. It's the silence that bothers you most: the silence of human things. There is noise enough— wind, and water, and the crashing of rocks as they are washed out of the ground they have held for centuries, then the horrifying whisper as they do not land but are swallowed up by some lake, unseen, below you. At first, you try to talk to yourself, to feel your own voice leaving you and echoing back, to establish inarguably your own concrete presence, a body in this place. But there is something awful about the sound of your words, the way they die into the world-noise, impermanent and unwelcome. So you are quiet, and as the world lets go of you, so you let go of it until you are a consciousness adrift on a ribbon of road, placeless and un-timed. *You have always suspected as much—that outside the limits of the life you knew there really was nothing at all.*

This you are sure of: when you stop the car at the top of some thin-aired summit to investigate the engine's new squeal and turn with the empty oilcan to take a look back, the first time in hours or days, what you see is, unmistakably, the view from your bedroom window. The image is so familiar to you, so deeply missed, that you cannot doubt what is in front of you and do not perceive in it any impossibility. You feel only a warm shock like waking from bad dreams to the comfort of your bed, a protecting arm wrapped around your shoulders. No matter the circumstances, this is always, somehow, the most likely view. You know full well what it means, but you cannot feel any horror in it: the two large pines that frame your vision, their branches spreading out over an emptiness, a fast-dropping bluff that falls into an endless, calm sea.

You have crossed the Great Divide, and now you dip downwards from the mountains and pour into the plains. With you comes the flood, welling over the peaks and staying suspended there for a moment to let you pass, impossible and incipient like a breath held too long, like water poised above the lip of an overfilled glass. You do not see the bubble breaking; there is no moment of absolute subsuming as you have expected, hoped for in the way we always hope for release, but instead you watch as the ditches beside the road become filled with a river that is faster than you, and stronger.

You watch as the ground ahead fills and pools as you descend towards it. As the ground grows flat, you feel a new tension in the wheel, a heavy pull and a low hum as you push through the deepening water.

For hours, you drive on through a wide and shallow lake punctuated by the tips of prairie grass and fences with eddies swirling at their posts—whirlpools pulling in the drowned bodies of a million beetles and flies. In the distance, sometimes, you see houses, the water climbing their steps and pushing in under their doors. You follow the road only by watching the yellow centerline; it is a few inches below but still reflects the light. When the sun begins to set, you realize that you will soon lose this guide too.

Still, it's shocking when it comes: the hard bump as you drop onto the lower ground and the high yowl of the tires as they burrow into the mud, kicking up red dirt and brown water onto your window and door. The engine runs for another few minutes, and this is the worst part because it really does sound like it's dying—not breaking but dying—and you've had it so long. *You can remember watching from the backseat as you mother put on makeup in the vanity mirror, swerving around potholes and fishtailing into the curves as she did. Still, you'd felt so safe.* Then the moaning turns to a quick, mechanical ticking, a dead battery click, and all the life is gone from it, so heavy a shell you can hardly believe it ever moved at all.

You feel a calmness pushing up in you, a deep, solid reconciliation. You would like nothing better than to lean your head against the window, to pull your knees up to your chest, and to sleep. Instead, you push your door open through the water that just touches its bottom edge and step out. This is not will but only some native vitality, some instinctual hatred of idleness. You pull open the trunk door and survey what you have kept with you so far, trying to decide what you can take. Finally, you take nothing at all. There is a relief in this. *The same as that of being told, as a little girl, that you had to clean your room, then spending the afternoon throwing everything away, assiduously erasing any trace of your having lived in that place at all.* Still, you cannot keep yourself from searching along the road as you walk and noting the mile-markers, making yourself the wild, reasonless promise that you will come back. You are not blind to your own devastation, but, as you go along, you catalog to yourself the things you see and feel, and the prime entries are fear; a disorienting blending of water, earth, and sky; cold; loneliness; and a glow of light on the horizon that you think may be electricity, and hence; hope. Loss hardly figures at all; all your world is washed in this same water, and as long as you are soaked in it, you have not lost anything, have not wandered far from home.

"You're salty," your father said to you once. You were walking in after a day at work and had not been near the water. "You always smell like salt." He said it like an accusation, and it had stayed with you, intimate and cruel. When Johnny had kissed you, years later, and said, "Like the Pacific," you did not know if that moment was ruined or the other saved.

In the center of the road, there is a passageway, a foot or so wide, straddling the yellow line, and this is mostly dry. You walk along this thin path, looking down into the water around you and feeling a silly pride, like shooting past a line of stopped traffic from the carpool lane.

"I'm really getting somewhere now," you say aloud and laugh. The sound of your voice does not bother you so much here. You feel a new expansiveness. You think that maybe you are just dissolving.

Your mother came into the house one morning, holding another pile of dead lilies in her gloved hands. You were eating breakfast and watched as bits of soil dropped onto the floor.

"The ground here eats the roots," she said. "It just eats them alive."

Your socks are wet, and the cold squelching of them bothers you so much that after a mile you stop and take them off. You carry your shoes, one in each hand. The cold smoothness of the pavement feels good on your bare feet, though after a mile or so more you realize they have begun to go numb and clumsy. You stop and stand on one foot, squeezing the other between your palms until you can no longer sense the difference between skin and skin, and then you switch. This doesn't help for very long, and by the time the second foot is warmed, the first has already begun to feel heavy and prickling. You wish now that you had taken a few things with you, at least—a dry pair of socks, a package of granola, a bottle of clean water—but you find it hard to regret that moment of decision and the brief high of bravery it brought you.

Now it is too late to go back anyway. Though travel across the flat expanse is slow and discouraging, you see for certain now that there is a town ahead, and that it has pulled itself an iota closer for your efforts. Still, you are growing tired, and you know there is only so long you can go on in the dark before you have to sleep, but there is nowhere to sleep—nowhere for miles and miles. This is a new sensation to you, this basic and incomprehensible lack of provisions, this utter inhospitableness. You decide again that you have made a mistake in leaving your home; you always had what you needed. *He's always said you were spoiled. Too spoiled to know how good you had it. But the word seemed wrong; you have often enough sliced into fruit gone by a day or two and loved the thickness—the earth—of its scent.*

You come to a place where the water gets deeper, or the land dips down low enough to submerge you if you go any farther. At the edge of this place, you let your legs fold under you, squatting, at first, to stretch the weak and puffed muscles of your back, then dropping to the wet ground, no longer concerned with staying warm or dry, so long as you can sit. In front of you is a river coursing fast and desperate, with earth, wood, and metal tumbling in its froth. You try to imagine what this place might have been before the flood: a rare valley in the plains, a sheltered lowland harboring bluebells and honeybees. *"This is my new favorite place,"* *Mara had said once, immersing her small, chubby legs in the water of a flower-choked* *stream. Your parents had taken you there to play and sat together on a small rise. This* *must have been the spring they left you.* Or maybe it was always a river; even so over-swelled, it has the look of a permanent thing. You think of the valley your mother lived in, the way it looked from the mountaintops, and you think that this flood is not something that rolled in but rather something that rose up, boiling out of the ground where it had always been. The experts know no more than you do, and you know only the slivers of what you've seen, but you do not believe this is ocean water you are soaked in. This is a native revolt and no invasion. *Walking on the beach, your father would* *pick up broken clamshells and throw them back into the water. "More dead soldiers,"* *he'd say, and you'd thought it must have been an awful war.*

The town sits on the other side of the river, down what you guess is a mile or two of dusty road. On you, the rain is still falling—light and indistinct, still soaking—but ahead you see a dryness so complete it crackles. A wind is blowing towards you. As it comes, it is whipping up little cyclones of red dirt and scattering them in the mud around you like a dusting of cinnamon. You can feel the grit on your face, swelling with the moisture it finds there. In the distance, you can hear traffic.

Among the loveliest sounds you have ever heard is the sound of your mother singing *Mara to sleep, her voice filtering down through the floorboards an hour before your own* *bedtime. Also, the crack of a sail changing shape with the wind, the bedsprings in* *Johnny's truck creaking when he sits down, traffic across the river, and the sound dirt* *makes when a big clod of it is pulled up with a shovel. You did not go to many Sunday-* *school classes when you were young, but in one you learned that the book of Psalms was* *not the book of Songs, and you were heartbroken.*

The roaring of water is all around you, rising up in front and creeping from behind. You turn and look, but there is nothing for the sound to bounce off—the legendary flatness of the plains. You wonder if you have made it to Kansas, after all. You look down at your hands, planted on the ground behind you, and see that they are underwater to the wrist. It is still moving in. You have come to the edge of the flood, and across the river is a different kind of world altogether. Though you see no reason to believe that this barrier will hold, no definite safety, the low glow of headlights moving between stop signs or gliding smooth along the unbroken eternity of country roads tells you that the people there are not afraid of the drowning that has tracked you across these miles. *You had expected for years to* *one day swim too far—to bob up to the surface of a swell and find yourself in the empty* *expanse of the ocean without bearing or safe passage home, to be given over completely to the water—but you had not expected this fight. You had not expected you would fight at all.*

You stand up and shake your arms, trying to feel the strength in them, but it isn't much. You pull your phone from your pocket, but the screen has gone green and fuzzed-out, the circuits awash. You wonder whom you would have called—what you would have said.

You think you would have called your mother. You don't have her number, but, if you did, you would have called and asked her if she and Steve got out all right. And maybe, if they had, you would ask if she wanted to make a different peace with you, would ask if she wanted to take everything back, if she wanted to come and get you, to take you home, to drive you back to the house you grew up in, to fish it out from the deep ends of the past and dry it, to have never left at all, to let you sit on her bed in the mornings, to do her dance-steps on the wooden floor, to swim in the ocean, to grow veiny plants in the back yard that die in the salt earth, and to stick there, to stay, no matter what. If she said yes to that, then you would turn back around and never have to look at that crossing again, would never have to wonder. But if she said no, if she didn't or couldn't answer, then you would have no choice.

She taught you to swim. It was her hands under your belly. It was her voice yelling, "Kick, Jane, kick."

Maybe you would call Mara too. Maybe you would tell her that you were both pretty young, and, if this all went well, you'd come out on the other side, soaked but drying, in a future that would eclipse this past two or three times over, or as many times as it took for you both to forget it, to wash your hands of it all. Maybe that was what this was all about, if only for the two of you: something that had become so dirty that it had to be washed clean, even if that meant it got washed away. She'd get angry when you said that because she was only just discovering how much she loved that dirt you both were born on, how even now it was in the cracks of her hands and the beds of her nails. She would not understand that you could feel the same way and still be so glad to see it sink. But maybe she would try, and maybe she would forgive you for the cruelty in your voice, and then you would swim across it, to her.

You were afraid, and your legs felt so weak and tired, like the cold of the water had gotten deep inside them.

To Johnny you would apologize, and if he did not know why or what for, that would make it easier—easier to know that your actions were what mattered in the life he wanted you for, not your words and mutinous thoughts, not the shiftless and unsettled interiors of your days. To come to him—doubting, ungrateful, and hungry, but just to come—would be enough.

She said, "Just keep kicking, Jane. I'm going to take my hands away." You yelled that you couldn't, and you begged her not to, but, of course, she did.

You would not call your father. You would not let the sound of the unanswered call reverberate in the silence of the line long enough to imagine the other end: the small room, cramped with his rubble, the leavings of him. The sound of the ringing phone would shake the water that pooled in the room, or pooled over it, forming ripples that would rise to the surface and spread out wide across the sea and the land. A quivering would pass through the waters of the world until it found you there, phone pressed to your ear, listening for the silence of him. The quiver would swirl around your ankles and splash onto your calves, exploring you like any other obstacle. Without you ever knowing, your blood would respond, taking up a sympathetic vibration, a tuning fork or an unbowed violin, humming out the harmony to the song. Maybe you would never feel it, but there it would be, inside of you: the things he could not answer for, the sound of his not answering.

You sank like a stone, but it was only the first time. You kicked.

You drop the phone on the bank of the river, knowing you do not need even that extra weight. The current is moving fast and strong, and you have the good sense to be afraid, but you know that if you do not go under, do not get dragged into the directionless below, you will be swept clear. You imagine yourself gasping on the opposite bank, drying in the dirt of that new place, and truly believe that you will make it there. You keep your eyes up above the water, and then you are wading, until you are swimming.

28433832R00065

Made in the USA
Charleston, SC
12 April 2014